WILLIAM TREVOR

MATILDA'S ENGLAND

PENGUIN BOOKS

PENGUIN BOOKS

Published by the Penguin Group. Penguin Books Ltd, 27 Wrights Lane, London w8 5tz, England. Penguin Books USA Inc., 375 Hudson Street, New York, New York 10014, USA. Penguin Books Australia Ltd, Ringwood, Victoria, Australia. Penguin Books Canada Ltd. 10 Alcorn Avenue, Toronto, Ontario, Canada m4v 3b2. Penguin Books (NZ) Ltd, 182–190 Wairau Road, Auckland 10, New Zealand   Penguin Books Ltd, Registered Offices: Harmondsworth, Middlesex, England · 'The Tennis Court' (1975) and 'The Summer-house' and 'The Drawing-room' (1978) have been taken from *The Collected Stories* of William Trevor, published by Penguin Books in 1993. This edition published 1995 · Copyright © William Trevor, 1975, 1978. All rights reserved · Typeset by Datix International Limited, Bungay, Suffolk. Printed in England by Clays Ltd, St Ives plc ·

CONTENTS

I

The Tennis Court

Old Mrs Ashburton used to drive about the lanes in a governess cart drawn by a donkey she called Trot. We often met her as we cycled home from school, when my brother and my sister were at the Grammar School and I was still at the village school. Of the three of us I was Mrs Ashburton's favourite, and I don't know why that was except that I was the youngest. 'Hullo, my Matilda,' Mrs Ashburton would whisper in her throaty, crazy-sounding way. 'Matilda,' she'd repeat, lingering over the name I so disliked, drawing each syllable away from the next. 'Dear Matilda.' She was excessively thin, rather tall, and frail-looking. We made allowances for her because she was eighty-one.

Usually when we met her she was looking for wild flowers, or if it was winter or autumn just sitting in her governess cart in some farmer's gateway, letting the donkey graze the farmer's grass. In spring she used to root out plants from the hedges with a little trowel. Most of them were weeds, my brother said; and looking back on it now, I realize that it wasn't for wild flowers, or weeds, or grazing for our donkey that she drove about the lanes. It was in order to meet us cycling back from school.

'There's a tennis court at Challacombe Manor,' she said one day in May, 1939. 'Any time you ever wanted to play, Dick.' She stared at my brother with piercing black eyes that were the colour of quality coal. She was eccentric, standing there in a long, very old and bald fur coat, stroking the ears of her donkey while he nibbled a hedge. Her hat was attached to her grey hair by a number of brass hat-pins. The hat was of faded green felt,

1

the hat-pins had quite large knobs at the ends of them, inlaid with pieces of green glass. Green, Mrs Ashburton often remarked, was her favourite colour, and she used to remove these hat-pins to show us the glass additions, emphasizing that they were valueless. Her bald fur coat was valueless also, she assured us, and not even in its heyday would it have fetched more than five pounds. In the same manner she remarked upon her summer hats and dresses, and her shoes, and the governess cart, and the donkey.

'I mean, Dick,' she said that day in 1939, 'it's not much of a tennis court, but it was once, of course. And there's a net stacked away in one of the outhouses. And a roller, and a marker. There's a lawn-mower, too, because naturally you'll need that.'

'You mean, we could play on your court, Mrs Ashburton?' my sister Betty said.

'Of course I mean that, my dear. That's just what I mean. You know, before the war we really did have marvellous tennis parties at Challacombe. Everyone came.'

'Oh, how lovely!' Betty was fourteen and Dick was a year older, and I was nine. Betty was fair-haired like the rest of us, but much prettier than me. She had very blue eyes and a wide smiling mouth that boys at the Grammar School were always trying to kiss, and a small nose, and freckles. Her hair was smooth and long, the colour of hay. It looked quite startling sometimes, shining in the sunlight. I used to feel proud of Betty and Dick when they came to collect me every afternoon at Mrs Pritchard's school. Dick was to leave the Grammar School in July, and on the afternoons of that warm May, as Betty and I cycled home with him, we felt sorry that he wouldn't be there

next term. But Dick said he was glad. He was big, as tall as my father, and very shy. He'd begun to smoke, a habit not approved of by my father. On the way home from school we had to stop and go into a ruined cottage so that he could have a Woodbine. He was going to work on the farm; one day the farm would be his.

'It would be lovely to play tennis,' Betty said.

'Then you must, my dear. But if you want to play this summer you'll have to get the court into trim.' Mrs Ashburton smiled at Betty in a way that made her thin, elderly face seem beautiful. Then she smiled at Dick. 'I was passing the tennis court the other day, Dick, and I suddenly thought of it. Now why shouldn't those children get it into trim? I thought. Why shouldn't they come and play, and bring their friends?'

'Yes,' Dick said.

'Why ever don't you come over to Challacombe on Saturday? Matilda, too, of course. Come for tea, all three of you.'

Mrs Ashburton smiled at each of us in turn. She nodded at us and climbed into the governess cart. 'Saturday,' she repeated.

'Honestly, Betty!' Dick glared crossly at my sister, as though she were responsible for the invitation. 'I'm not going, you know.'

He cycled off, along the narrow, dusty lane, big and red-faced and muttering. We followed him more slowly, talking about Mrs Ashburton. 'Poor old thing!' Betty said, which was what people round about often said when Mrs Ashburton was mentioned, or when she was seen in her governess cart.

The first thing I remember in all my life was my father breaking a fountain-pen. It was a large black-and-white pen, like tortoise-shell or marble. That was the fashion for fountain-pens then: two or three colours marbled together, green and black, blue and   3 white, red and black-and-white. Conway Stewart, Waterman's, Blackbird. Propelling pencils were called Eversharp.

The day my father broke his pen I didn't know all that: I learnt it afterwards, when I went to school. I was three the day he broke the pen. 'It's just a waste of blooming money!' he shouted. He smashed the pen across his knee while my mother anxiously watched. Waste of money or not, she said, it wouldn't help matters to break the thing. She fetched him the ink and a dip-pen from a drawer of the dresser. He was still angry, but after a minute or two he began to laugh. He kissed my mother, pulling her down on to the knee he'd broken the pen over. Dick, who must have been nine then, didn't even look up from his homework. Betty was there too, but I can't remember what she was doing.

The kitchen hasn't changed much. The old range has gone, but the big light-oak dresser is still there, with the same brass handles on its doors and drawers and the same Wedgwood-blue dinner-set on its shelves, and cups and jugs hanging on hooks. The ceiling is low, the kitchen itself large and rectangular, with the back stairs rising from the far end of it, and a door at the bottom of them. There are doors to the pantry and the scullery, and to the passage that leads to the rest of the house, and to the yard. There's a long narrow light-oak table, with brass handles on its drawers, like the dresser ones, and oak chairs that aren't as light as all the other oak because chairs darken with use. But the table isn't scrubbed once a week any more, and the brass doesn't gleam. I know, because now and again I visit the farmhouse.

I remember the kitchen with oil-lamps, and the time, the day after my fifth birthday, when the men came to wire the house for electricity. My mother used to talk about an Aga, and often when she took us shopping with her she'd bring us to Archers', the builders' merchants, to look at big cream-coloured Agas. After a time, Mr Gray of the Aga department didn't even bother to bustle up to her when he saw her coming. She'd stand there, plump and pink-cheeked, her reddish hair neat beneath the brim of her hat, touching the display models, opening the oven doors and lifting up the two big hot-plate covers. When we returned to the farmhouse my father would tease her, knowing she'd been to Archers' again. She'd blush, cutting ham at teatime or offering round salad. My father would then forget about it. 'Well, I'm damned,' he'd say, and he'd read out an item from the weekly paper, about some neighbouring farmer or new County Council plans. My mother would listen and then both of them would nod. They were very good friends, even though my father teased her. She blushed like a rose, he said: he teased her to see it.

Once, before the electricity came, I had a nightmare. It was probably only a few months before, because when I came crying down to the kitchen my father kept comforting me with the reminder that it would soon be my fifth birthday. 'You'll never cry then, Matilda,' he whispered to me, cuddling me to him. 'Big girls of five don't cry.' I fell asleep, but it's not that that I remember now, not the fear from the nightmare going away, or the tears stopping, or my father's caressing: it's the image of my parents in the kitchen as I stumbled down the back stairs. There were two oil-lamps lit and the fire in the range was glowing red-hot behind its curved bars, and the heavy black kettle wasn't quite singing. My father was asleep with last Saturday's weekly paper on his knees, my mother was reading one of the books from the bookcase in the dining-room we never used, probably *The Garden of Allah*, which was her favourite. The two sheepdogs were asleep under the table, and when I opened the door at the 5 top of the stairs they both barked because they knew that at that particular time no one should be opening that door. 'Oh, now, now,' my mother said, coming to me, listening to me when I said that there were cows on my bedroom wall. I remember the image of the two of them because they looked so happy sitting there, even though my mother hadn't got her Aga, even though my father was sometimes worried about the farm.

Looking back on it now, there was a lot of happiness, although perhaps not more than many families experience. Everything seems either dismal or happy in retrospect, and the happiness in the farmhouse is what I think of first when ever I think now of that particular past. I remember my mother baking in the kitchen, flour all over her plump arms, and tiny beads of moisture on her forehead, because the kitchen was always hot. I remember my father's leathery skin and his smile, and the way he used to shout at the sheepdogs, and the men, Joe and Arthur, sitting on yellow stubble, drinking tea out of a bottle, on a day hay had been cut.

Our farm had once been the home-farm of Challacombe Manor, even though our farmhouse was two miles away from the manor house. There'd been servants and gardeners at Challacombe Manor then, and horses in the stables, and carriages coming and going. But the estate had fallen into rack and ruin after the First World War because Mr Ashburton hadn't been able to keep it going and in the end, in 1924, he'd taken out various mortgages. When he died, in 1929, the extent of his debts was so great that Mrs Ashburton had been obliged to let Lloyd's Bank foreclose on the mortgages, which is how it came about that my father bought Challacombe Farm. It was a tragedy, people round about used to say, and the real tragedy was that Mr Ashburton had come back from the war in such a strange state that he hadn't minded about everywhere falling into rack and ruin. According to my father, Lloyd's Bank owned Challacombe Manor itself and had granted Mrs Ashburton permission to live there in her lifetime. It wouldn't surprise him, my father said, if it turned out that Lloyd's Bank owned Mrs Ashburton as well. 'He drank himself to death,' people used to say about Mr Ashburton. 'She watched him and didn't have the heart to stop him.' Yet before the First World War Mr Ashburton had been a different kind of man, energetic and sharp. The Challacombe estate had been a showpiece.

To me in particular Mrs Ashburton talked about her husband. She was lucky that he'd come back from the war, even if he hadn't been able to manage very well. His mind had been affected, she explained, but that was better than being dead. She told me about the men who'd died, gardeners at Challacombe Manor, and the farm workers on the estate, and the men she and her husband had known in the town. 'I thanked God,' Mrs Ashburton said, 'when he came safely back here all in one piece. Everything fell to bits around us, but it didn't matter because at least he was still alive. You understand, Matilda?'

I always nodded, although I didn't really understand. And then she'd go on about the estate as it had been, and then about her husband and the conversations they used to have. Sometimes she didn't address me directly. She smiled and just talked, always returning to the men who had been killed and how lucky she was that her husband had at least come back. She'd prayed, she said, that he'd come back, and every time another man from the estate or from the neighbourhood had been reported dead she'd felt that there was a better chance that her husband wouldn't die also. 'By the law of averages,' she explained, 'some had to come back. Some men have always come back from wars, you convince yourself.'

At this point I would always nod again, and Mrs Ashburton would say that looking back on it now she felt ashamed that she had ever applied the law of averages to the survival or death of men. Doing so was as horrible as war itself: the women who were left at home became cruel in their fear and their selfishness. Cruelty was natural in war, Mrs Ashburton said.

At the time she'd hated the Germans and she was ashamed of that too, because the Germans were just people like other people. But when she talked about them the remains of the hatred were still in her voice, and I imagined the Germans from what she told me about them: people who ate black bread and didn't laugh much, who ate raw bacon, who were dour, grey and steely. She described the helmets they wore in wartime. She told me what a bayonet was, and I used to feel sick when I thought of one going into a man's stomach and being twisted in there to make sure the man would die. She told me about poison gas, and the trenches, and soldiers being buried alive. The way she spoke I knew she was repeating, word for word, the things her husband had told her, things that had maybe been the cause of his affected mind. Even her voice sounded unusual when she talked about the war, as though she was trying to imitate her husband's voice, and the terror that had been in it. He used to cry, she said, as he walked about the gardens, unable to stop the tears once they'd begun.

Dick didn't say anything while we rode the two miles over to Challacombe Manor that Saturday. He didn't even say anything when he suddenly dismounted and leaned his bicycle against a black gate, and climbed over the gate to have a smoke behind the hedge. If my father had come by he'd have known what was happening because he would have seen Betty and myself waiting in the lane, surrounded by the cloud of smoke that Dick always managed to make with his Woodbine. Our job was to warn him if we saw my father coming, but my father didn't come that afternoon and when Dick had finished we continued on our way.

We'd often been to tea at Challacombe Manor before. Mrs Ashburton said we were the only visitors she had because most of her friends were dead, which was something that happened, she explained, if you were eighty-one. We always had tea in the kitchen, a huge room that smelt of oil, with armchairs in it and a wireless, and an oil-stove on which Mrs Ashburton cooked, not wishing to have to keep the range going. There were oatcakes for tea, and buttered white and brown bread, and pots of jam that Mrs Ashburton bought in the town, and a cake she bought also, usually a fruitcake. Afterwards we'd walk through the house with her, while she pointed out the places where the roof had given way, and the dry rot, and windows that were broken. She hadn't lived in most of the house since the war, and had lived in even less of it since her husband had died in 1929. We knew these details by heart because she'd told us so many times. In one of the outhouses there was an old motor-car with flat tyres, and the gardens were now all overgrown with grass and weeds. Rhododendrons were choked, and buddleia and kerria and hydrangeas.

The house was grey and square with two small wings, a stone Georgian house with wide stone steps leading to a front door that had pillars on either side of it and a fanlight above it. The gravel expanse in front of it was grassy now, and slippery in wet weather because of moss that had accumulated. French windows opened on to it on either side of the hall door, from the rooms that had been the drawing-room and the dining-room. Lawns stretched around the house, with grass like a meadow on them now. The tennis court, which we'd never known about until Mrs Ashburton mentioned it, was hidden away, beyond the jungle of shrubbery.

'You see?' she said. 'You see, Dick?' She was wearing a long, old-fashioned dress and a wide-brimmed white hat, and sunglasses because the afternoon was fiercely bright.

The grass on the tennis court was a yard high, as high as the rusty iron posts that were there to support the net. 'Look,' Mrs Ashburton said.

She led us to the stable-yard, past the outhouse where the motor-car was, and into a smaller outhouse. There was a lawn-mower there, as rusty as the tennis posts, and a marker in the same condition, and an iron roller. Tucked into the beams above our heads was a rolled-up tennis net. 'He adored tennis,' she said. 'He really loved it.'

She turned and we followed her across the stable-yard, into the kitchen by the back door. She talked about her husband while she made tea.

We ate the bought fruitcake, listening to her. We'd heard it all before, but we always considered it was worth it because of the cake and the biscuits and the buttered bread and the pots of jam. And always before we left she gave us ginger beer and pieces of chocolate broken up on a saucer. She told us about the child which might have been born to her husband and herself, six months after the old queen died, but which had miscarried. 'Everything went wrong,' she said. She told us about the parties there'd been at Challacombe Manor. Champagne and strawberries and cream, and parties with games that she described, and fancy dress.

'No reason at all,' she said, 'why we shouldn't have a tennis party.'

Dick made a sighing sound, a soft, slight noise that Mrs Ashburton didn't hear.

'Tennis party?' Betty murmured.

'No reason, dear.'

That morning Dick and Betty had had an argument. Betty 'had said that of course he must go to tea with Mrs Ashburton, since he'd always gone in the past. And Dick had said that Mrs Ashburton had been cunning: all these years, he said, she'd been inviting us to tea so that when the time was ripe she could get us to clean up her old tennis court. 'Oh, don't be silly!' Betty had cried, and then had said that it would be the cruellest thing that Dick had ever done if he didn't go to tea with an old woman just because she'd mentioned her tennis court. I'd been cross with Dick myself, and none of us felt very happy because the matter of the tennis court had unattractively brought into the open the motive behind our putting up with Mrs Ashburton. I didn't like it when she called me her Matilda and put her arms around me, and said she was sure her child would have been a little girl, and that she was almost as sure that she'd have called her Matilda. I didn't like it when she went on and on about the war and her husband coming back a wreck, or about the champagne and the strawberries and cream. 'Poor Mrs Ashburton!' we'd always said, but it wasn't because she was poor Mrs Ashburton that we'd filled the emptiness of Saturday afternoons by cycling over to Challacombe Manor.

'Shall we go and have another look at it?' she said when we'd eaten all the food that was on the table. She smiled in her frail, almost beautiful way, and for a moment I wondered if Dick wasn't perhaps right about her cunning. She led the way back to the overgrown tennis court and we all four stood looking at it.

'It's quite all right to smoke, Dick,' Mrs Ashburton said, 'if you want to.'

Dick laughed because he didn't know how else to react. He'd gone as red as a sunset. He kicked at the rusty iron tennis post, and then as casually as he could he took a packet of squashed Woodbines from his pocket and began to fiddle with a box of matches. Betty poked him with her elbow, suggesting that he should offer Mrs Ashburton a cigarette.

'Would you like one, Mrs Ashburton?' Dick said proffering the squashed packet.

'Well, you know, I think I would, Dick.' She laughed and took the cigarette, saying she hadn't smoked a cigarette since 1915. Dick lit it for her. Some of the matches fell from the matchbox on to the long grass. He picked them up and replaced them, his own cigarette cocked out of the corner of his mouth. They looked rather funny, the two of them, Mrs Ashburton in her big white hat and sunglasses.

'You'd need a scythe,' Dick said.

That was the beginning of the tennis party. When Dick walked over the next Saturday with a scythe, Mrs Ashburton had a packet of twenty Player's waiting for him. He scythed the grass and got the old hand-mower going. The stubble was coarse and by the time he'd cut it short there were quite large patches of naked earth, but Betty and Mrs Ashburton said they didn't matter. The court would do as it was for this summer, but in the spring, Dick said, he'd put down fresh grass-seed. It rained heavily a fortnight later, which was fortunate, because Dick was able to even out some of the bumps with the roller. Betty helped him, and later on she helped him mark the court out. Mrs Ashburton and I watched, Mrs Ashburton holding my hand and often seeming to imagine that I was the child which hadn't been born to her.

We took to going to Challacombe Manor on Sunday mornings as well as Saturdays. There were always packets of Craven A, and ginger beer and pieces of chocolate. 'Of course, it's not her property,' my father said whenever anyone mentioned the tennis court, or the net that Mrs Ashburton had found rolled up in an outhouse. At dinnertime on Sundays, when we all sat around the long table in the kitchen, my father would ask Dick how he'd got on with the court. He'd then point out that the tennis court and everything that went with it was the property of Lloyd's Bank. Every Sunday dinnertime we had the same roast beef and roast potatoes and Yorkshire pudding, and carrots or brussels sprouts according to the seasonal variation, and apple pie and cream.

Dick didn't ever say much when my father asked him about the tennis court. 'You want to be careful, lad,' my father used to say, squashing roast potatoes into gravy. 'Lloyd's is strict, you know.' My father would go on for ages, talking about Lloyd's Bank or the Aga cooker my mother wanted, and you never quite knew whether he was being serious or not. He would sit there with his jacket on the back of his chair, not smiling as he ate and talked. Farmers were like that, my mother once told Betty when Betty was upset by him. Farmers were cautious and watchful and canny. He didn't at all disapprove of what Betty and Dick and Mrs Ashburton were doing with the tennis court, my mother explained, rather the opposite; but he was right when he reminded them that everything, including the house itself, was the property of Lloyd's Bank.

Mrs Ashburton found six tennis racquets in presses, which were doubtless the property of Lloyd's Bank also. Dick examined them and said they weren't too bad. They had an antiquated look, and the varnish had worn off the frames, but only two of them had broken strings. Even those two, so Dick said, could be played with. He and Mrs Ashburton handed the racquets to one another, blowing at the dust that had accumulated on the presses and the strings. They lit up their cigarettes, and Mrs Ashburton insisted on giving Dick ten shillings to buy tennis balls with.

I sat with Mrs Ashburton watching Dick and Betty playing their first game on the court. The balls bounced in a peculiar way because in spite of all the rolling there were still hollows and bumps on the surface. The grass wasn't green. It was a brownish yellow, except for the bare patches, which were ochre-coloured. Mrs Ashburton clapped every time there was a rally, and when Dick had beaten Betty 6–1, 6–4, he taught me how to hit the ball over the net, and how to volley it and keep it going. 'Marvellous, Matilda!' Mrs Ashburton cried, in her throaty voice, applauding again. 'Marvellous!'

We played all that summer, every Saturday and Sunday until the end of term, and almost every evening when the holidays came. We had to play in the evenings because at the end of term Dick began to work on the farm. 'Smoke your cigarettes if you want to,' my father said the first morning of the holidays, at breakfast. 'No point in hiding it, boy.' Friends of Dick's and Betty's used to come to Challacombe Manor to play also, because that was what Mrs Ashburton wanted: Colin Gregg and Barbara Hosell and Peggy Goss and Simon Turner and Willie Beach.

Sometimes friends of mine came, and I'd show them how to do it, standing close to the net, holding the racquet handle in the middle of the shaft. Thursday, August 31st, was the day Mrs Ashburton set for the tennis party: Thursday because it was half-day in the town.

Looking back on it now, it really does seem that for years and years she'd been working towards her tennis party. She'd hung about the lanes in her governess cart waiting for us because we were the children from the farm, the nearest children to Challacombe Manor. And when Dick looked big and strong enough and Betty of an age to be interested, she'd made her bid, easing matters along with fruitcake and cigarettes. I can imagine her now, on her own in that ruin of a house, watching the grass grow on her tennis court and watching Dick and Betty growing up and dreaming of one more tennis party at Challacombe, a party like there used to be before her husband was affected in the head by the Kaiser's war.

'August the 31st,' Betty reminded my parents one Sunday at dinnertime. 'You'll both come,' she said fiercely, blushing when they laughed at her.

'I hear Lloyd's is on the rampage,' my father said laboriously. 'Short of funds. Calling everything in.'

Dick and Betty didn't say anything. They ate their roast beef, pretending to concentrate on it.

''Course they're not,' my mother said.

'They'll sell Challacombe to some building fellow, now that it's all improved with tennis courts.'

'Daddy, don't be silly,' Betty said, blushing even more. All three of us used to blush. We got it from my mother. If my father blushed you wouldn't notice.

'True as I'm sitting here, my dear. Nothing like tennis courts for adding a bit of style to a place.'

Neither my mother nor my father had ever seen the tennis court. My father wouldn't have considered it the thing, to go walking over to Challacombe Manor to examine a tennis court. My mother was always busy, cooking and polishing brass. 15

Neither my father nor my mother knew the rules of tennis. When we first began to play Betty used to draw a tennis court on a piece of paper and explain.

'Of course we'll come to the tennis party,' my mother said quietly. 'Of course, Betty.'

In the middle of the tennis party, my father persisted, a man in a hard black hat from Lloyd's Bank would walk on to the court and tell everyone to go home.

'Oh, Giles, don't be silly now,' my mother said quite sharply, and added that there was such a thing as going on too much. My father laughed and winked at her.

Mrs Ashburton asked everyone she could think of to the tennis party, people from the farms round about and shopkeepers from the town. Dick and Betty asked their friends and their friends' parents, and I asked Belle Frye and the Gorrys and the Seatons. My mother and Betty made meringues and brandy-snaps and fruitcakes and Victoria sponge cakes and scones and buns and shortbread. They made sardine sandwiches and tomato sandwiches and egg sandwiches and ham sandwiches. I buttered the bread and whipped up cream and wrapped the plates of sandwiches in damp teacloths. Dick cleared a place in the shrubbery beside the tennis court and built a fire to boil kettles on. Milk was poured into bottles and left to keep cool in the larder. August 31st was a fine, hot day.

At dinnertime my father pretended that the truck which was to convey the food, and us too, to the tennis court had a broken carburettor. He and Joe had been working on it all morning, he said, but utterly without success. No one took any notice of him.

I remember, most of all, what they looked like. Mrs Ashburton
16 thin as a rake in a long white dress and her wide-brimmed white

hat and her sunglasses. My father in his Sunday clothes, a dark blue suit, his hair combed and his leathery brown face shining because he had shaved it and washed it specially. My mother had powder on her cheeks and her nose, and a touch of lipstick on her lips, although she didn't usually wear lipstick and must have borrowed Betty's. She was wearing a pale blue dress speckled with tiny white flowers. She'd spent a fortnight making it herself, for the occasion. Her reddish hair was soft and a little unruly, being freshly washed. My father was awkward in his Sunday suit, as he always was in it. His freckled hands lolled uneasily by his sides, or awkwardly held tea things, cup and saucer and plate. My mother blushed beneath her powder, and sometimes stammered, which she did when she was nervous.

Betty was beautiful that afternoon, in a white tennis dress that my mother had made her. Dick wore long white flannels that he'd been given by old Mr Bowe, a solicitor in the town who'd been to other tennis parties at Challacombe Manor but had no further use for white flannel trousers, being seventy-two now and too large for the trousers he'd kept for more than fifty years. My mother had made me a tennis dress, too, but I felt shy that day and didn't want to do anything except hand round plates of meringues and cake. I certainly didn't want to play, for the tennis was serious: mixed doubles, Betty and Colin Gregg against Dick and Peggy Goss, and Simon Turner and Edie Turner against Barbara Hosell and Willie Beach.

People were there whom my father said he hadn't seen for years, people who had no intention of playing tennis, any more than he had. Between them, Dick and Betty and Mrs Ashburton had cast a wide net, and my father's protests at the mounds of food that had been prepared met with their answer as car after car drew up, and dog-carts and pony and traps. Belle Frye and I 17 passed around the plates of meringues, and people broke off in their conversations to ask us who we were. Mrs Ashburton had spread rugs on the grass around the court, and four white ornamental seats had been repainted by Dick the week before. 'Just like the old days,' a man called Mr Race said, a corn merchant from the town. My mother nervously fidgeted, and I could feel her thinking that perhaps my father's laborious joke would come true, that any moment now the man from Lloyd's Bank would arrive and ask people what on earth they thought they were doing, playing tennis without the Bank's permission.

But that didn't happen. The balls zipped to and fro across the net, pinging off the strings, throwing up dust towards the end of the afternoon. Voices called out in exasperation at missed shots, laughter came and went. The sun continued to shine warmly, the tennis players wiped their foreheads with increasing regularity, the rugs on the grass were in the shade. Belle Frye and I collected the balls and threw them back to the servers. Mr Bowe said that Dick had the makings of a fine player.

Mrs Ashburton walked among the guests with a packet of Player's in her hand, talking to everyone. She kept going up to my mother and thanking her for everything she'd done. Whenever she saw me she kissed me on the hair. Mr Race said she shook hands like a duchess. The rector, Mr Throataway, laughed jollily.

At six o'clock, just as people were thinking of going, my father surprised everyone by announcing that he had a barrel of beer and a barrel of cider in the truck. I went with him and there they were, two barrels keeping cool beneath a tarpaulin, and two wooden butter-boxes full of glasses that he'd borrowed from the Heart of Oak. He drove the truck out from beneath the shade of the trees and backed it close to the tennis court. He and Dick set

18

the barrels up and other men handed round the beer and cider, whichever anyone wanted. 'Just like him,' I heard a woman called Mrs Garland saying. 'Now, that's just like him.'

It was a quarter to ten that evening before they stopped playing tennis. You could hardly see the ball as it swayed about from racquet to racquet, looping over the net, driven out of court. My father and Mr Race went on drinking beer, and Joe and Arthur, who'd arrived after milking, stood some distance away from them, drinking beer also. Mrs Garland and my mother and Miss Sweet and Mrs Tissard made more tea, and the remains of the sandwiches and cakes were passed around by Belle Frye and myself. Joe said he reckoned it was the greatest day in Mrs Ashburton's life. 'Don't go drinking that cider now,' Joe said to Belle Frye and myself.

We all sat around in the end, smacking at midges and finishing the sandwiches and cakes. Betty and Colin Gregg had cider, and you could see from the way Colin Gregg kept looking at Betty that he was in love with her. He was holding her left hand as they sat there, thinking that no one could see because of the gloom, but Belle Frye and I saw, all right. Just before we went home, Belle Frye and I were playing at being ghosts round at the front of the house and we came across Betty and Colin Gregg kissing behind a rhododendron bush. They were lying on the grass with their arms tightly encircling one another, kissing and kissing as though they were never going to stop. They didn't even know Belle Frye and I were there. 'Oh, Colin!' Betty kept saying. 'Oh, Colin, Colin!'

We wanted to say goodbye to Mrs Ashburton, but we couldn't find her. We ran around looking everywhere, and then Belle Frye suggested that she was probably in the house.

'Mrs Ashburton!' I called, opening the door that led from the stable-yard to the kitchen. 'Mrs Ashburton!'

It was darker in the kitchen than it was outside, almost pitch-dark because the windows were so dirty that even in daytime it was gloomy.

'Matilda,' Mrs Ashburton said. She was sitting in an armchair by the oil-stove. I knew she was because that was where her voice came from. We couldn't see her.

'We came to say goodbye, Mrs Ashburton.'

She told us to wait. She had a saucer of chocolate for us, she said, and we heard her rooting about on the table beside her. We heard the glass being removed from a lamp and then she struck a match. She lit the wick and put the glass back. In the glow of lamplight she looked exhausted. Her eyes seemed to have receded, the thinness of her face was almost sinister.

We ate our chocolate in the kitchen that smelt of oil, and Mrs Ashburton didn't speak. We said goodbye again, but she didn't say anything. She didn't even nod or shake her head. She didn't kiss me like she usually did, so I went and kissed her instead. The skin of her face felt like crinkled paper.

'I've had a very happy day,' she said when Belle Frye and I had reached the kitchen door. 'I've had a lovely day,' she said, not seeming to be talking to us but to herself. She was crying, and she smiled in the lamplight, looking straight ahead of her. 'It's all over,' she said. 'Yet again.'

We didn't know what she was talking about and presumed she meant the tennis party. 'Yet again,' Belle Frye repeated as we crossed the stable-yard. She spoke in a soppy voice because she was given to soppiness. 'Poor Mrs Ashburton!' she said, beginning to cry herself, or pretending to. 'Imagine being eighty-one,' she said. 'Imagine sitting in a kitchen and remembering all the other tennis parties, knowing you'd have to die soon. Race you,' Belle Frye said, forgetting to be soppy any more.

Going home, Joe and Arthur sat in the back of the truck with Dick and Betty. Colin Gregg had ridden off on his bicycle, and Mr Bowe had driven away with Mrs Tissard beside him and Mr Tissard and Miss Sweet in the dickey of his Morris Cowley. My mother, my father and myself were all squashed into the front of the truck, and there was so little room that my father couldn't change gear and had to drive all the way to the farm in first. In the back of the truck Joe and Arthur and Dick were singing, but Betty wasn't, and I could imagine Betty just sitting there, staring, thinking about Colin Gregg. In Betty's bedroom there were photographs of Clark Gable and Ronald Colman, and Claudette Colbert and the little Princesses. Betty was going to marry Colin, I kept saying to myself in the truck. There'd be other tennis parties and Betty would be older and would know her own mind, and Colin Gregg would ask her and she'd say yes. It was very beautiful, I thought, as the truck shuddered over the uneven back avenue of Challacombe Manor. It was as beautiful as the tennis party itself, the white dresses and Betty's long hair, and everyone sitting and watching in the sunshine, and evening slowly descending. 'Well, that's the end of that,' my father said, and he didn't seem to be talking about the tennis party because his voice was too serious for that. He repeated a conversation he'd had with Mr Bowe and one he'd had with Mr Race, but I didn't listen because his voice was so lugubrious, not at all like it had been at the tennis party. I was huddled on my mother's knees, falling asleep. I imagined my father was talking about Lloyd's Bank again, and I could hear my mother agreeing with him.

I woke up when my mother was taking off my dress in my bedroom.

'What is it?' I said. 'Is it because the tennis party's over? Why's everyone so sad?'

My mother shook her head, but I kept asking her because she was looking sorrowful herself and I wasn't sleepy any more. In the end she sat on the edge of my bed and said that people thought there was going to be another war against the Germans.

'Germans?' I said, thinking of the grey, steely people that Mrs Ashburton had so often told me about, the people who ate black bread.

It would be all right, my mother said, trying to smile. She told me that we'd have to make special curtains for the windows so that the German aeroplanes wouldn't see the lights at night. She told me there'd probably be sugar rationing.

I lay there listening to her, knowing now why Mrs Ashburton had said that yet again it was all over, and knowing what would happen next. I didn't want to think about it, but I couldn't help thinking about it: my father would go away, and Dick would go also, and Joe and Arthur and Betty's Colin Gregg. I would continue to attend Miss Pritchard's school and then I'd go on to the Grammar, and my father would be killed. A soldier would rush at my father with a bayonet and twist the bayonet in my father's stomach, and Dick would do the same to another soldier, and Joe and Arthur would be missing in the trenches, and Colin Gregg would be shot.

My mother kissed me and told me to say my prayers before I went to sleep. She told me to pray for the peace to continue, as she intended to do herself. There was just a chance, she said, that it might.

She went away and I lay awake, beginning to hate the Germans and not feeling ashamed of it, like Mrs Ashburton was. No German would ever have played tennis that day, I thought, no German would have stood around having tea and sandwiches and meringues, smacking away the midges when night came. No

German would ever have tried to recapture the past, or would have helped an old woman to do so, like my mother and my father had done, and Mr Race and Mr Bowe and Mr Throataway and Mrs Garland, and Betty and Dick and Colin Gregg. The Germans weren't like that. The Germans wouldn't see the joke when my father said that for all he knew Lloyd's Bank owned Mrs Ashburton.

I didn't pray for the peace to continue, but prayed instead that my father and Dick might come back when the war was over. I didn't pray that Joe and Arthur and Colin Gregg should come back since that would be asking too much, because some men had to be killed, according to Mrs Ashburton's law of averages. I hadn't understood her when Mrs Ashburton had said that cruelty was natural in wartime, but I understood now. I understood her law of averages and her sitting alone in her dark kitchen, crying over the past. I cried myself, thinking of the grass growing on her tennis court, and the cruelty that was natural.

2

The Summer-house

My father came back twice to the farm, unexpectedly, without warning. He walked into the kitchen, the first time one Thursday morning when there was nobody there, the second time on a Thursday afternoon.

My mother told us how on the first occasion she'd been crossing the yard with four eggs, all that the hens had laid, and how she'd sensed that something was different. The sheepdogs weren't in the yard, where they usually were at this time. Vaguely she'd thought that that was unusual. Hours later, when Betty and Dick and I came in from school, our parents were sitting at the kitchen table, talking. He was still in his army uniform. The big brown teapot was on the table, and two cups with the dregs of tea in them, and bread on the bread-board, and butter and blackberry jam. There was a plate he'd eaten a fry from, with the marks of egg-yolk on it. Even now it seems like yesterday. He smiled a slow, teasing smile at us, as though mocking the emotion we felt at seeing him there, making a joke even of that. Then Betty ran over to him and hugged him. I hugged him too. Dick stood awkwardly.

The second time he returned he walked into the kitchen at half past four, just after I'd come in from school. I was alone, having my tea.

'Hullo, Matilda,' he said.

I was nearly eleven then. Betty was sixteen and Dick was seventeen. Dick wasn't there that second time: he'd gone into the army himself. Betty had left the Grammar School and was helping my mother to keep the farm going. I was still at Miss Pritchard's.

I was going to be pretty, people used to say, although I couldn't see it myself. My hair had a reddish tinge, like my mother's, but it was straight and uninteresting. I had freckles, which I hated, and my eyes were a shade of blue I didn't much care for either. I detested being called Matilda. Betty and Dick, I considered, were much nicer names, and Betty was beautiful now. My friend Belle Frye was getting to be beautiful also. She claimed to have Spanish blood in her, though it was never clear where it came from. Her hair was jet-black and her skin, even in the middle of winter, was almost as deeply brown as her eyes. I'd have loved to look like her and to be called Belle Frye, which I thought was a marvellous name.

I made my father tea that Thursday afternoon and I felt a bit shy because I hadn't seen him for so long. He didn't comment on my making the tea, although he might have said that I hadn't been able to before. Instead he said he hadn't had a decent cup of tea since he'd been home the last time. 'It's great to be home, Matilda,' he said.

A few weeks later my mother told me he was dead. She told me at that same time of day and on a Thursday also: a warm June afternoon that had been tiring to trudge home from school through.

'Belle Frye has to stay in for two hours,' I was saying as I came into the kitchen. My mother told me to sit down.

The repetition was extraordinary, the three Thursday afternoons. That night in bed I was aware of it, lying awake thinking about him, wondering if he'd actually been killed on a Thursday also.

All the days of the week had a special thing about them: they had different characters and even different colours. Monday was light brown, Tuesday black, Wednesday grey, Thursday orange, Friday yellow, Saturday purplish, Sunday white. Tuesday was a day I liked because we had double History, Friday was cosy, Saturday I liked best of all. Thursday would be special now: I thought that, marking the day with my grief, unable to cry any more. And then I remembered that it had been a Thursday afternoon when old Mrs Ashburton had invited everyone for miles round to her tennis party, when I had realized for the first time that there was going to be a war against the Germans: Thursday, 31 August 1939.

I would have liked there to be a funeral, and I kept thinking about one. I never mentioned it to my mother or to Betty, or asked them if my father had had a funeral in France. I knew he hadn't. I'd heard him saying they just had to leave you there. My mother would cry if I said anything about it.

Then Dick came back, the first time home since he'd joined the army. He'd been informed too, and time had passed, several months, so that we were all used to it by now. It was even quite like the two occasions when my father had returned. Dick telling stories about the army. We sat in the kitchen listening to him, huddled round the range, with the sheepdogs under the table, and when the time came for him to go away I felt as I'd felt when my father had gone back. I knew that Betty and my mother were thinking about Dick in that way, too: I could feel it, standing in the yard holding my mother's hand.

Colin Gregg, who'd kissed Betty at Mrs Ashburton's tennis party, came to the farm when he was home on leave. Joe and Arthur, who'd worked for my father on the farm, came also. At one time or another they all said they were sorry about my father's death, trying not to say it when I was listening, lowering their voices, speaking to my mother.

Two years went by like that. Dick still came back, and Colin Gregg and Joe and Arthur. I left Miss Pritchard's school and went to the Grammar School. I heard Betty confiding to my mother that she was in love with Colin Gregg, and you could see it was Colin Gregg being in the war that she thought about now, not Dick. Belle Frye's father had had his left arm amputated because of a wound, and had to stay at home after that. A boy who'd been at the Grammar School, Roger Laze, had an accident with a gun when he was shooting rabbits, losing half his left foot. People said it was a lie about the rabbit-shooting. They said his mother had shot his foot off so that he wouldn't have to go into the army.

At church on Sundays the Reverend Throataway used to pray for victory and peace, and at school there was talk about the Russians, and jokes about Hitler and Göring and most of all about Goebbels. I remembered how old Mrs Ashburton used to talk about the previous war, from which her husband had come back with some kind of shell-shock. She'd made me think of Germans as being grey and steely, and I hated them now, just as she had. Whenever I thought about them I could see their helmets, different from the helmets of English soldiers, protecting their necks as well as their heads. Whenever I thought of the time before the war I thought of Mrs Ashburton, who had died soon after she'd given her tennis party. On the way home from school I'd sometimes go into the garden of Challacombe Manor and stand there looking at the tall grass on the tennis court, remembering all the people who'd come that afternoon, and how they'd said it was just like my father to say the tennis party was a   27 lot of nonsense and then to bring on beer and cider at the end of the day. The tennis party had been all mixed up with our family. It felt like the last thing that had happened before the war had begun. It was the end of our being as we had been in our farmhouse, just as in the past, after the previous war, there must have been another end: when the farm had ceased to be the home-farm of Challacombe Manor, when the estate had been divided up after Mrs Ashburton's husband hadn't been able to run it any more.

When I wandered about the overgrown garden of Challacombe Manor I wondered what Mr Ashburton had been like before the war had affected him, but I couldn't quite see him in my mind's eye: all I could see was the person Mrs Ashburton had told me about, the silent man who'd come back, who hadn't noticed that everything was falling into rack and ruin around him. And then that image would disappear and I'd see my father instead, as he'd been in the farmhouse. I remembered without an effort the brown skin of his arms and his brown, wide forehead and the way crinkles formed at the sides of his eyes. I remembered his hands on the kitchen table at mealtimes, or holding a newspaper. I remembered his voice saying there'd been frost. 'Jack Frost's been,' he used to say.

When I was twelve I began to pray a lot. I prayed that my father should be safe in heaven and not worried about us. I prayed that Dick should be safe in the war, and that the war would soon end. In Scripture lessons the Reverend Throataway used to explain to us that God was in the weeds and the insects, not just in butterflies and flowers. God was involved in the worst things we did as well as our virtues, he said, and we drove another thorn into His beloved son's head when we were wicked. I found that difficult to understand. I looked at weeds and insects, endeavouring to imagine God's presence in them but not succeeding. I asked Belle Frye if she could, but she giggled and said God was a carpenter called Joseph, the father of Jesus Christ. Belle Frye was silly and the Reverend Throataway so vague and complicated that his arguments about the nature of God seemed to me like foolish chatter. God was neither a carpenter nor a presence in weeds and insects. God was a figure in robes, with a beard and shreds of cloud around Him. The paradise that was mentioned in the Bible was a garden with tropical plants in it, through which people walked, Noah and Moses and Jesus Christ and old Mrs Ashburton. I could never help thinking that soon the Reverend Throataway would be there too: he was so old and frail, with chalk on the black material of his clothes, sometimes not properly shaved, as if he hadn't the energy for it. I found it was a consolation to imagine the paradise he told us about, with my own God in it, and to imagine Hitler and Göring and Goebbels, with flames all around them, in hell. The more I thought about it all and prayed, the closer I felt to my father. I didn't cry when I thought about him any more, and my mother's face wasn't all pulled down any more. His death was just a fact now, but I didn't ever want not to feel close to him. It was as if being close to him was being close to God also, and I wanted that so that God could answer my prayer about keeping Dick safe in the war. I remembered how Mrs Ashburton had worked it out that by the law of averages some men have to come back from a war, and I suggested to the robed figure in charge of the tropical paradise that in all fairness our family did not deserve another tragedy. With my eyes tightly closed, in bed at night or suddenly stopping on the journey to school, I repetitiously prayed that Dick would be alive to come back when the war was over. That was all I asked for in the end because I could feel that my father was safe in the eternal life that the Reverend Throataway spoke of, and I didn't ask any more that the war should be over soon in case I was asking too much. I never told anyone about my prayers and I was never caught standing still with my eyes closed on the way to school. My father used to smile at me when I did that and I could faintly hear his voice teasing Dick about his smoking or teasing my mother about the Aga cooker she wanted, or Betty about almost anything. I felt it was all right when he smiled like that and his voice came back. I felt he was explaining to me that God had agreed to look after us now, provided I prayed properly and often and did not for a single instant doubt that God existed and was in charge. Mrs Ashburton had been doubtful about that last point and had told me so a few times, quite frightening me. But Mrs Ashburton would be in possession of the truth now, and would be forgiven.

My thoughts and my prayers seemed like a kind of world to me, a world full of God, with my father and Mrs Ashburton in their eternal lives, and the happiness that was waiting for the Reverend Throataway in his. It was a world that gradually became as important as the reality around me. It affected everything. It made me different. Belle Frye was still my friend, but I didn't like her the way I once had.

One wet afternoon she and I clambered into Challacombe Manor through a window that someone had smashed. We hadn't been there since the night of the tennis party, when we'd found Mrs Ashburton crying and she'd given us pieces of chocolate. We'd run out into the night, whispering excitedly about an old woman crying just because a party was over. I wouldn't have believed it then if someone had said I'd ever think Belle Frye silly.

'Whoever's going to live here?' she whispered in the dank hall after we'd climbed through the window. 'D'you think it'll just fall down?'

'There's a mortgage on it. Lloyd's Bank have it.'

'What's that mean then?'

'When the war's finished they'll sell the house off to someone else.'

All the furniture in the drawing-room had been taken away, stored in the cellars until someone, some day, had time to attend to it. People had pulled off pieces of the striped red wallpaper, boys from the Grammar School probably. There were names and initials and dates scrawled on the plaster. Hearts with arrows through them had been drawn.

'Anyone could come and live here,' Belle Frye said.

'Nobody'd want to.'

We walked from room to room. The dining-room still had a sideboard in it. There was blue wallpaper on the walls: none of that had been torn off, but there were great dark blots of damp on it. There were bundled-up newspapers all over the floor, and empty cardboard boxes that would have been useless for anything because they'd gone soft due to the damp. Upstairs there was a pool of water on a landing and in one of the bedrooms half the ceiling had fallen down. Everywhere there was a musty smell.

'It's haunted,' Belle Frye said.

'Of course it isn't.'

'She died here, didn't she?'

'That doesn't make it haunted.'

'I can feel her ghost.'

I knew she couldn't. I thought she was silly to say it, pretending about ghosts just to set a bit of excitement going. She said it again and I didn't answer.

We crawled out again, through the broken window. We   31

wandered about in the rain, looking in the outhouses and the stables. The old motor-car that used to be in one of them had been taken away. The iron roller that Dick had rolled the tennis court with was still there, beside the tennis court itself.

'Let's try in here,' Belle Frye said, opening the door of the summer-house.

All the times I'd come into the garden on my own I'd never gone into the summer-house. I'd never even looked through a window of Challacombe Manor itself, or poked about the outhouses. I'd have been a bit frightened, for even though I thought it was silly of Belle Frye to talk about ghosts it wouldn't have surprised me to see a figure moving in the empty house or to hear something in one of the stables, a tramp maybe or a prisoner escaped from the Italian prisoner-of-war camp five miles away. The Italians were black-haired men mostly, whom we often met being marched along to a road to work in the fields. They always waved and were given to laughing and singing. But even so I wouldn't have cared to meet one on his own.

In the centre of the summer-house was the table that had been covered with a white cloth, with sandwiches and cakes and the tea-urn on it, for the tennis party. The tennis marker was in a corner, placed there by Dick, I suppose, after he'd marked the court. The net was beside it, and underneath it, almost hidden by it, were two rugs, one of them brown and white, a kind of Scottish tartan pattern, the other grey. Both of these rugs belonged in our farmhouse. Could they have been lying in the summer-house since the tennis party? I wondered. I couldn't remember when I'd seen them last.

Facing one another across the table were two chairs which I remembered being there on the day of the party. They were dining-room chairs with red plush seats, brought from the house with a dozen or so others and arrayed on one side of the tennis court so that people could watch the games in comfort. These two must have been left behind when the others had been returned. I was thinking about that when I remembered my father hurriedly putting them into the summer-house at the end of the day. 'It'll maybe rain,' he'd said.

'Hey, look,' Belle Frye said. She was pointing at an ashtray on the table, with cigarette-butts and burnt-out matches in it. 'There's people using this place,' she said giggling. 'Maybe an escaped prisoner,' she suggested, giggling again.

'Maybe.' I said it quickly, not wanting to pursue the subject. I knew the summer-house wasn't being used by an escaped prisoner. Our rugs hadn't been there since the day of the tennis party. They were part of something else, together with the cigarette-butts and the burnt-out matches. And then, quite abruptly, it occurred to me that the summer-house was where Betty and Colin Gregg came when Colin Gregg was on leave: they came to kiss, to cuddle one another like they'd been cuddling in the rhododendrons after the tennis party. Betty had brought the rugs specially, so that they could be warm and comfortable.

'I bet you it's an Eye-tie,' Belle Frye said. 'I bet you there's one living here.'

'Could be.'

'I'm getting out of it.'

We ran away. We ran through the overgrown garden on that wet afternoon and along the lane that led to the Fryes' farm. I should have turned in the opposite direction after we'd left the garden, but I didn't: I went with her because I didn't want her silliness to spoil everything. I thought it was romantic, Betty and Colin Gregg going to the summer-house. I remembered a film   33 called *First Love*, which Betty had gone on about. It had Deanna Durbin in it.

'I'm going to tell,' Belle Frye said, stopping for breath before we came to the Fryes' farmyard. Her eyes jangled with excitement. There were drops of moisture in her smooth black hair.

'Let's have it a secret, Belle.'

'He could murder you, a blooming Eye-tie.'

'It's where my sister and Colin Gregg go.' I had to say it because I knew she'd never be able to keep a secret that involved an Italian prisoner of war. I knew that even if no prisoner had escaped people would go to the summer-house to see for themselves. I knew for a fact, I said, that it was where Betty and Colin Gregg went, and if she mentioned it to anyone I'd tell about going into Challacombe Manor through a broken window. She'd said as we'd clambered through it that her father would murder her if he knew. He'd specifically told her that she mustn't go anywhere near the empty house because the floorboards were rotten and the ceilings falling down.

'But why would you tell?' she cried, furious with me. 'What d'you want to tell for?'

'It's private about the summer-house. It's a private thing of Betty's.'

She began to giggle. We could watch, she whispered. We could watch through the window to see what they got up to. She went on giggling and whispering and I listened to her, not liking her. In the last year or so she'd become like that, repeating the stories she heard from the boys at school, all to do with undressing and peeping. There were rhymes and riddles and jokes that she repeated also, none of them funny. She'd have loved peeping through the summer-house window.

34   'No,' I said. 'No.'

'But we could. We could wait till he was home on leave. We needn't make a sound.' Her voice had become shrill. She was cross with me again, not giggling any more. Her eyes glared at me. She said I was stupid, and then she turned and ran off. I knew she'd never peep through the summer-house window on her own because it wasn't something you could giggle over when you were alone. And I knew she wouldn't try and persuade anyone to go with her because she believed me when I said I'd tell about breaking into Challacombe Manor. Her father was a severe man; she was, fortunately, terrified of him.

I thought about the summer-house that evening when I was meant to be learning a verse of 'The Lady of Shalott' and writing a composition, 'The Worst Nightmare I Ever Had'. I imagined Betty and Colin Gregg walking hand in hand through the overgrown garden and then slipping into the summer-house when it became dusky. A summer's evening it was, with pink in the sky, and the garden was scented with the blossoms of its shrubs. I imagined them sitting on the two dining-chairs at the table, Colin telling her about the war while he smoked his cigarettes, and Betty crying because he would be gone in twelve hours' time and Colin comforting her, and both of them lying down on the rugs so that they could be close enough to put their arms around each other.

In the kitchen while I tried to record the details of a nightmare all I could think about was the much pleasanter subject of my sister's romance. She was in the kitchen also. She'd changed from her farm-working clothes into a navy-blue skirt and a matching jersey. I thought she was more beautiful than usual. She and my mother were sitting on either side of the range, both of them knitting, my mother reading a book by A.J. Cronin at the same time, my sister 35 occasionally becoming lost in a reverie. I knew what she was thinking about. She was wondering if Colin Gregg was still alive.

Months went by and neither he nor Dick came back. There were letters, but there were also periods when no letters arrived and you could feel the worry, for one of them or the other. The war was going to be longer than everyone had thought. People looked gloomy sometimes, and when I caught their gloom I imagined bodies lying unburied and men in aeroplanes, with goggles on, the aeroplanes on fire and the men in goggles burning to death. Ages ago France had been beaten, and I remembered that in a casual moment in a Scripture class the Reverend Throataway had said that that could never happen, that the French would never give in. We would never give in either, Winston Churchill said, but I imagined the Germans marching on the lanes and the roads and through the fields, not like the cheerful Italians. The Germans were cruel in their helmets and their grey steeliness. They never smiled. They knew you hated them.

Belle Frye would have thought I was mad if I'd told her any of that, just like she'd have thought I was mad if I'd mentioned about praying and keeping my father vivid in my mind. She was the first friend I'd ever had, but the declining of our friendship seemed almost natural now. We still sat next to one another in class, but we didn't always walk home together. Doing that had always meant that one of us had to go the long way round and avoiding this extra journey now became an excuse. Not having had Dick and Betty to walk home with for so long, I'd enjoyed Belle Frye's company, but now I found myself pretending to be in a hurry or just slipping away when she wasn't looking. She didn't seem to mind, and we still spent days together, at the weekends or in the holidays. We'd have tea in each other's kitchens, formally invited by our mothers, who didn't realize that we weren't such friends. And that was still quite nice.

Sometimes in the evenings my mother used to go to see a woman called Mrs Latham because Mrs Latham was all alone in the Burrow Farm, three miles away. On these occasions I always hoped Betty would talk to me about Colin Gregg, that she'd even mention the summer-house. But she never did. She'd sit there knitting, or else writing a letter to him. She'd hear me say any homework I had to learn by heart, a theorem or poetry or spelling. She'd make me go to bed, just like my mother did, and then she'd turn on the wireless and listen to *Monday Night at Eight* or *Waterlogged Spa* or *Itma*. She'd become very quiet, less impatient with me than she'd been when we were younger, more grown-up, I suppose. I often used to think about her on those nights when my mother was out, when she was left alone in the kitchen listening to the wireless. I used to feel sorry for her.

And then, in that familiar sudden way, Colin Gregg came back on leave.

That was the beginning of everything. The evening after he came back was a Saturday, an evening in May. I'd been at the Fryes' all afternoon and when we'd finished tea we played cards for an hour or so and then Mrs Frye said it was time for me to go home. Belle wanted to walk with me, even though we'd probably have walked in silence. I was glad when her father said no. It was too late and in any case he had to go out himself, to set his rabbit snares: he'd walk with me back to our farm. I said goodbye, remembering to thank Mrs Frye, and with his remaining arm Mr Frye pushed his bicycle on the road beside me. He didn't talk at all. He was completely different from my father, 37 never making jokes or teasing. I was quite afraid of him because of his severity.

The sheepdogs barked as I ran across our yard and into the kitchen. My mother had said earlier that she intended to go over to see Mrs Latham that evening. By eight o'clock Betty and Colin Gregg were to be back from the half past four show at the pictures, so that I wouldn't be in the house alone. It was twenty past eight now, and they weren't there.

I ran back into the yard, wanting to tell Mr Frye, but already he'd cycled out of sight. I didn't at all like the idea of going to bed in the empty house.

I played with the dogs for a while and then I went to look at the hens, and then I decided that I'd walk along the road to meet Betty and Colin Gregg. I kept listening because at night you could always hear the voices of people cycling in the lanes. I kept saying to myself that my mother wouldn't want me to go to bed when there was no one in the farmhouse. It was very still, with bits of red in the sky. I took the short-cut through the garden of Challacombe Manor and I wasn't even thinking about Betty and Colin Gregg when I saw two bicycles in the shrubbery at the back of the summer-house. I didn't notice them at first because they were almost entirely hidden by rhododendron bushes. They reminded me of the rugs half hidden beneath the tennis net.

Colin Gregg was going away again on Monday. He was being sent somewhere dangerous, he didn't know where, but I'd heard Betty saying to my mother that she could feel in her bones it was dangerous. When my mother had revealed that she intended to visit Mrs Latham that evening I'd said to myself that she'd arranged the visit so that Colin Gregg and Betty could spend the evening on their own in our kitchen. But on the way back from the pictures they'd gone into the summer-house, their special place.

Even now I can't think why I behaved like Belle Frye, unable to resist something. It was silly curiosity, and yet at the time I think it may have seemed more than just that. In some vague way I wanted to have something nice to think about, not just my imagining the war, and my prayers for Dick's safety and my concern with people's eternal lives. I wanted to see Betty and Colin Gregg together. I wanted to feel their happiness, and to see it.

It was then, while I was actually thinking that, that I realized something was the matter. I realized I'd been stupid to assume they could take the short-cut through the garden: you couldn't take the short-cut if you were coming from the town on a bicycle because you had to go through fields. You'd come by the lanes, and if you wanted to go to the summer-house you'd have to turn back and go there specially. It seemed all wrong that they should do that when they were meant to be back in the farmhouse by eight o'clock.

I should have turned and gone away. In the evening light I was unable to see the bicycles clearly, but even so I was aware that neither of them was Betty's. They passed out of my sight as I approached one of the summer-house's two small windows.

I could see nothing. Voices murmured in the summer-house, not saying anything, just quietly making sounds. Then a man's voice spoke more loudly, but I still couldn't hear what was being said. A match was struck and in a sudden vividness I saw a man's hand and a packet of Gold Flake cigarettes on the table, and then I saw my mother's face. Her reddish hair was untidy and she was smiling. The hand that had been on the table put a cigarette between her lips and another hand held the match to it. 39

I had never in my life seen my mother smoking a cigarette before.

The match went out and when another one was struck it lit up the face of a man who worked in Blow's drapery. My mother and he were sitting facing one another at the table, on the two chairs with the red plush seats.

Betty was frying eggs at the range when I returned to the kitchen. Colin Gregg had had a puncture in his back tyre. They hadn't even looked yet to see if I was upstairs. I said we'd all forgotten the time at the Fryes', playing cards.

In bed I kept remembering that my mother's eyes had been different, not like they'd been for a long time, two dark-blue sparks. I kept saying to myself that I should have recognized her bicycle in the bushes because its mudguards were shaped like a V, not rounded like the mudguards of modern bicycles.

I heard Colin and Betty whispering in the yard and then the sound of his bicycle as he rode away and then, almost immediately, the sound of my mother's bicycle and Betty saying something quietly and my mother quietly replying. I heard them coming to bed, Betty first and my mother twenty minutes later. I didn't sleep, and for the first time in my life I watched the sky becoming brighter when morning began to come. I heard my mother getting up and going out to do the milking.

At breakfast-time it was as though none of it had happened, as though she had never sat on the red plush chair in the summer-house, smoking cigarettes and smiling at a man from a shop. She ate porridge and brown bread, reading a book: *Victoria Four-thirty* by Cecil Roberts. She reminded me to feed the hens and she asked Betty what time Colin Gregg was coming over. Betty said any minute now and began to do the washing up. When Colin Gregg came he mended one of the cow-house doors.

That day was horrible. Betty tried to be cheerful, upset because Colin Gregg was being sent to somewhere dangerous. But you could feel the effort of her trying and when she thought no one was looking, when my mother and Colin were talking to one another, her face became unhappy. I couldn't stop thinking about my father. Colin Gregg went back to the war.

A month went by. My mother continued to say she was going to see Mrs Latham and would leave Betty and me in the kitchen about once a week.

'Whatever's the matter with Matilda?' I heard Betty saying to her once, and later my mother asked me if I had a stomach ache. I used to sit there at the table trying to understand simultaneous equations, imagining my mother in the summer-house, the two bicycles half hidden in the bushes, the cigarettes and the ashtray.

'The capital of India,' I would say. 'Don't tell me; I know it.'

'Begins with a "D",' Betty would prompt.

He came to the kitchen one evening. He ate cabbage and baked potatoes and fish pie, chewing the cabbage so carefully you couldn't help noticing. He was scrawny, with a scrawny nose. His teeth were narrowly crowded, his whole face pulled out to an edge, like a chisel. His hair was parted in the middle and oiled. His hands were clean, with tapering fingers. I was told his name but I didn't listen, not wishing to know it.

'Where'd you get the fish?' he asked my mother in a casual way. His head was cocked a little to one side. He was smiling with his narrow teeth, making my mother flustered as she used to get in the past, when my father was alive. She was even beginning to blush, not that I could see a cause for it. She said:

'Betty, where did you get the cod?'

'Croker's,' Betty said.

Betty smiled at him and my mother said quickly that Croker's were always worth trying in case they'd got any fish in, although of course you could never tell. It sounded silly the way she said it.

'I like fish,' he said.

'We must remember that.'

'They say it's good for you,' Betty said.

'I always liked fish,' the man said. 'From a child I've enjoyed it.'

'Eat it up now,' my mother ordered me.

'Don't you like fish, Matilda?' he said.

Betty laughed. 'Matilda doesn't like lots of things. Fish, carrots, eggs. Semolina. Ground rice. Custard. Baked apples, gravy, cabbage.'

He laughed, and my mother laughed. I bent my head over the plate I was eating from. My face had gone as hot as a fire.

'Unfortunately there's a war on,' he said. 'Hard times, Matilda.'

I considered that rude. It was rude the way he'd asked where the fish had come from. He was stupid, as well. Who wanted to hear that he liked fish? He was a fool, like Stupid Miller, who'd been at Miss Pritchard's school. He was ridiculous-looking and ugly, with his pointed face and crushed-together teeth. He'd no right to say there was a war on since he wasn't fighting in it.

They listened to the news on the wireless and afterwards they listened to the national anthems of the countries which were fighting against Germany. He offered my mother and Betty cigarettes and they both took one. I'd never seen Betty smoking a cigarette before. He'd brought a bottle of some kind of drink with him. They drank it sitting by the range, still listening to the national anthems.

'Good-night, Matilda,' he said, standing up when my mother told me it was time to go to bed. He kissed me on the cheek and I could feel his damp teeth. I didn't move for a moment after he'd done that, standing quite close to him. I thought I was going to bring up the fish pie and if I did I wanted to cover his clothes with it. I wouldn't have cared. I wouldn't have been embarrassed.

I heard Betty coming to bed and then I lay for hours, waiting for the sound of his bicycle going away. I couldn't hear their voices downstairs, the way I'd been able to hear voices when Betty had been there. Betty's had become quite loud and she'd laughed repeatedly. I guessed they'd been playing cards, finishing off the bottle of drink he'd brought. When I'd been there Betty had suggested rummy and he'd said that not a drop of the drink must be left. He'd kept filling up Betty's and my mother's glasses, saying the stuff was good for you.

I crossed the landing to the top of the stairs that led straight down into the kitchen. I thought they must have fallen asleep by the range because when a board creaked beneath my feet no one called out. I stood at the turn of the narrow staircase, peering through the shadows at them.

Betty had taken one of the two lamps with her as she always did. The kitchen was dim, with only the glow from the other. On the table, close to the lamp, was the bottle and one of the glasses they'd drunk from. The two dogs were stretched in front of the range. My mother was huddled on the man's knee. I could see his tapering fingers, one hand on the material of her dress, the other stroking her hair. While I watched he kissed her, bending his damp mouth down to her lips and keeping it there. Her eyes were closed but 43 his were open, and when he finished kissing her he stared at her face.

I went on down the stairs, shuffling my bare feet to make a noise. The dogs growled, pricking up their ears. My mother was half-way across the kitchen, tidying her hair with both hands, murmuring at me.

'Can't you sleep, love?' she said. 'Have you had a dream?'

I shook my head. I wanted to walk forward, past her to the table. I wanted to pick up the bottle he'd brought and throw it on to the flags of the floor. I wanted to shout at him that he was ugly, no more than a half-wit, no better than Stupid Miller, who hadn't been allowed in the Grammar School. I wanted to say no one was interested in his preference for fish.

My mother put her arms around me. She felt warm from sitting by the range, but I hated the warmth because it had to do with him. I pushed by her and went to the sink. I drank some water even though I wasn't thirsty. Then I turned and went upstairs again.

'She's sleepy,' I heard my mother say. 'She often gets up for a drink when she's sleepy. You'd better go, dear.'

He muttered something else and my mother said that they must have patience.

'One day,' she said. 'After it's all over.'

'It'll never end.' He spoke loudly, not muttering any more. 'This bloody thing could last for ever.'

'No, no, my dear.'

'It's all I want, to be here with you.'

'It's what I want too. But there's a lot in the way.'

'I don't care what's in the way.'

'We have to care, dear.'

44   'I love you,' he said.

'My own darling,' my mother said.

She was the same as usual the next day, presumably imagining that being half-asleep I hadn't noticed her sitting on the man's knees and being kissed by his mouth. In the afternoon I went into the summer-house. I looked at the two plush-seated chairs, imagining the figures of my mother and the man on them. I carried the chairs, one by one, to an outhouse and up a ladder to a loft. I put the tennis net underneath some seed-boxes. I carried the two rugs to the well in the cobbled yard and dropped them down it. I returned to the summer-house, thinking of doing something else, I wasn't sure what. There was a smell of stale tobacco, coming from butts in the ashtray. On the floor I found a tie-pin with a greyhound's head on it and I thought the treacherous, ugly-looking dog suited him. I threw it into the rhododendron shrubbery.

'Poor chap,' I heard Betty saying that evening. 'It's a horrid thing to have.' She'd always noticed that he looked delicate, she added.

'He doesn't get enough to eat,' my mother said.

In spite of her sympathy, you could see that Betty wasn't much interested in the man: she was knitting and trying to listen to *Bandwagon*. As far as Betty was concerned he was just some half-sick man whom my mother felt sorry for, the way she was supposed to feel sorry for Mrs Latham of Burrow Farm. But my mother wanted to go on talking about him, with a pretended casualness. It wasn't the right work for a person who was tubercular, she said, serving in a shop.

I imagined him in Blow's, selling pins and knitting-needles and satin by the yard. I thought the work suited him in the same way as the greyhound's-head tie-pin did.

'What's it mean, tubercular?' I asked Belle Frye, and she said it meant you suffered from a disease in your lungs.

'I expect you could fake it.'

'What'd you want to do that for?'

'To get out of the war. Like Mrs Laze shot off Roger Laze's foot.'

'Who's faking it then?'

'That man in Blow's.'

I couldn't help myself: I wanted it to be known that he was faking a disease in his lungs. I wanted Belle Frye to tell people, to giggle at him in Blow's, pointing him out. But in fact she wasn't much interested. She nodded, and then shrugged in a jerky way she had, which meant she was impatient to be talking about something else. You could tell she didn't know the man in Blow's had become a friend of my mother's. She hadn't seen them on their bicycles; she wouldn't have wanted to change the subject if she'd looked through the summer-house window and seen them with their cigarettes. Before that I hadn't thought about her finding out, but now I wondered if perhaps she would some time, and if other people would. I imagined the giggling and the jokes made up by the boys in the Grammar School, and the severity of Mr Frye, and the astonishment of people who had liked my father.

I prayed that none of that would happen. I prayed that the man would go away, or die. I prayed that my mother would be upset again because my father had been killed in the war, that she would remember the time when he had been in the farmhouse with us. I prayed that whatever happened she would never discredit him by allowing the man from Blow's to be there in the farmhouse, wearing my father's clothes.

Every day I prayed in the summer-house, standing close to

the table with my eyes closed, holding on to the edge of it. I went there specially, and more vividly than ever I could see my father in the tropical garden of his eternal life. I could see old Mrs Ashburton walking among the plants with her husband, happy to be with him again. I could see the bearded face of the Almighty I prayed to, not smiling but seeming kind.

'Oh, my God,' was all my mother could say, whispering it between her bursts of tears. 'Oh, my God.'

Betty was crying too, but crying would do no good. I stood there between them in the kitchen, feeling I would never cry again. The telegram was still on the table, its torn envelope beside it. It might have said that Dick was coming home on leave, or that Colin Gregg was. It looked sinister on the table because Dick was dead.

I might have said to my mother that it was my fault as well as hers. I might have said that I'd known I should pray only for Dick to be safe and yet hadn't been able to prevent myself from asking, also, that she'd be as she used to be, that she wouldn't ever marry the man from Blow's.

But I didn't say that. I didn't say I'd prayed about the man, I just said it was a Thursday again.

'Thursday?' my mother whispered, and when I explained she didn't understand. She hadn't even noticed that the two times my father had come home it had been a Thursday and that the tennis party had been on a Thursday and that the other telegram had come on a Thursday too. She shook her head, as if denying all this repetition, and I wanted to hurt her when she did that because the denial seemed to be part and parcel of the summer-house and the man from Blow's. More deliberately than a moment ago I again didn't confess that I had ceased to concentrate on Dick's safety in my prayers. Instead I said that in a war against the Germans you couldn't afford to take chances, you couldn't go kissing a man when your husband had been killed.

'Oh, my God,' my mother said again.

Betty was staring at her, tears still coming from her eyes, bewildered because she'd never guessed about my mother and the man.

'It has nothing to do with this,' my mother whispered. 'Nothing.'

I thought Betty was going to attack my mother, maybe hammer at her face with her fists, or scratch her cheeks. But she only cried out, shrieking like some animal caught in a trap. The man was even married, she shrieked, his wife was away in the Women's Army. It was horrible, worse than ever when you thought of that. She pointed at me and said I was right: Dick's death was a judgement, things happened like that.

My mother didn't say anything. She stood there, white-faced, and then she said the fact that the man was married didn't make anything worse.

She spoke to Betty, looking at her, not at me. Her voice was quiet. She said the man intended to divorce his wife when the war came to an end. Of course what had happened wasn't a judgement.

'You won't marry him now,' Betty said, speaking as quietly.

My mother didn't reply. She stood there by the table and there was a silence. Then she said again that Dick's death and the man were two different things. It was terrible, she said, to talk as we were talking at a time like this. Dick was dead: that was the only thing that mattered.

'They used to go to the summer-house,' I said. 'They had two of our rugs there.'

My mother turned her head away, and I wanted Betty to remember as I was remembering and I believe she did. I could sense her thinking of the days when my father was alive, when Dick used to smoke cigarettes on the way home from school, when we were all together in the farmhouse, not knowing we were happy. That time seemed to haunt the kitchen just then, as if my mother was thinking about it too, as if our remembering had willed it back.

'He could never come here now,' Betty said to my mother. 'You couldn't do it to Matilda.'

I didn't know why she should have particularly mentioned me since it concerned us all, and anyway I felt it was too late to bother about me. Too much had happened. I felt I'd been blown to pieces, as if I'd been in the war myself, as if I'd been defeated by it, as old Mrs Ashburton had been defeated by the war. The man would come to live in the farmhouse. He would wear my father's clothes. He would sit by the range, reading the newspaper. He would eat at the table, and smile at me with his narrow teeth.

My mother left the kitchen. She went upstairs and after a few minutes we heard her sobbing in her bedroom. Sobbing would do no good, I thought, any more than crying would.

I walked by myself through the fields. Dick's death wasn't the same as my father's. There was the same emptiness and the same feeling that I never wanted to eat anything again or to drink anything again, but it was different because this was the second time. Dick was dead and we'd get used to it: that was something I knew now.

I didn't cry and I didn't pray. Praying seemed nonsense as I walked through the fields; praying was as silly as Belle Frye's thinking that God was a carpenter or the Reverend Throataway saying God was in the weeds. God wasn't like that in the least. He wasn't there to listen to what you prayed for. God was something else, something harder and more awful and more frightening.

I should have known that the man from Blow's would be married, that he'd have a wife who was helping in the war while he was going on about a disease. It was somehow all of a piece with Betty wanting to hit my mother, and Mrs Laze shooting off her son's foot so that he could stay alive, and God being frightening. Facts and images rattled in my mind, senselessly jumbled, without rhyme or reason. Dick was there too, dead and unburied in his uniform, something ordinary to get used to.

I sat in the sunshine on a bank that had primroses on it. I could have returned to the farmhouse and let my mother put her arms around me, but I continued to sit there, still not crying, remembering Mrs Ashburton saying that cruelty in wartime was natural. At the time I hadn't understood what she'd meant, but I could feel the cruelty she'd spoken of now. I could feel it in myself, in my wanting my mother to be more unhappy than I was. Dick's death was more bearable because she could be blamed, as Betty had blamed her in speaking of a judgement.

3
The Drawing-room

I am writing this in the drawing-room, in fact at Mrs Ashburton's writing-desk. I don't think of it as a story – and certainly not as a letter, for she can never read it – but as a record of what happened in her house after the war. If she hadn't talked to me so much when I was nine there would not be this record to keep, and I would not still feel her presence. I do not understand what has happened, but as I slowly move towards the age she was when she talked to me I slowly understand a little more. What she said has haunted me for thirty-nine years. It has made me old before my time, and for this I am glad. I feel like a woman of sixty; I'm only forty-eight.

In 1951 the house was bought by people called Gregary. 'Filthy rich,' my stepfather said.

My stepfather had just been made manager at Blow's drapery in the town. He used to drive off every day in a blue pre-war baby Ford, and I was always glad to see him go. I worked on the farm with Joe and Arthur, like my father had, like my brother Dick would have if he hadn't been killed in the desert offensive.

I thought it was typical of my stepfather to know that the Gregarys were rich. It was the kind of information he picked up in Blow's, conversing across his counter, the gossip enlivening his chisel face. He said Mr Gregary was a businessman involved in the manufacturing of motor-car components. He'd made a killing during the war: my stepfather called him a post-war tycoon.

On my twenty-first birthday my mother insisted on giving a kind of party. We had it in the farmhouse kitchen. We cooked a turkey and a ham and my mother made a great fuss about the vegetables that had been my favourites when I was small: celery and parsnips and carrots, and roast potatoes. The carrots were to be in a parsley sauce, the parsnips roasted with the potatoes. We made trifle because trifle had been a childhood favourite also, and brandy-snaps. It was impossible not to recall the preparations for Mrs Ashburton's tennis party on the Thursday before the war, but of course I didn't mention that. My mother believed that I didn't want to live in the present. I often felt her looking at me and when I turned my head I could see for a moment, before she changed her expression, that she believed I dwelt far too much on times that were not our own.

Fifteen people came to my birthday party, not counting my mother and my stepfather and myself. My sister Betty, who had married Colin Gregg, came with her two children. Belle Frye had married Martin Draper, who'd inherited the mill at Bennett's Cross: they brought the baby that had made the marriage necessary. Mr and Mrs Frye were there, and Miss Pritchard, who'd taught us all at school. Joe and Arthur, and Joe's wife, Maudie, came; and Mrs Laze and her son Roger. The idea was, I believe, that I might one day marry Roger, but it wasn't a prospect I relished. He limped because of his foot, and he hardly ever spoke, being shy like his mother. I didn't dislike him, I just didn't want to marry him.

All the time I kept wishing my mother hadn't given this party. It made me think of my other birthdays. Not that there was any reason to avoid doing that, except that naturally the past seemed better, especially the distant past, before the war. Miss Pritchard was the only person I ever talked to about things like that. 'Come and talk to me whenever you want to, Matilda,' she'd said one day in 1944, and ever since I'd been visiting her in her tiny sitting-room, knowing she was lonely because she was retired now. In a way our conversations reminded me of my conversations with Mrs Ashburton, except that it was Mrs Ashburton, not I, who used to do the talking and half the time I hadn't understood her. It was I who'd suggested that Miss Pritchard should come to my birthday party. I'd heard my mother saying to my stepfather that she couldn't understand it: she thought it extraordinary that I didn't want to invite lots of the boys I'd been at the Grammar School with, that I didn't want to have a gramophone going and tables of whist. My stepfather said he didn't think people played whist like they used to. He stood up for me, the way he always did, even though he didn't know I was listening. He made such efforts and still I couldn't like him.

Seventeen of us sat down at the kitchen table at half past six and my stepfather poured out cider for us, and orangeade for Betty's children. Belle Frye's baby was put to sleep upstairs. I couldn't think of her as Belle Draper, and haven't ever been able to since. Martin Draper had been a silly kind of boy at school and he still was silly now.

My stepfather carved the turkey and my mother the ham. Everyone was talking about Challacombe Manor having been sold to the people called Gregary.

'The son's going to run the place,' my stepfather said. 'Tax fiddle, I dare say.'

You could see that Miss Pritchard didn't know what he was talking about, and you could see that she suspected he didn't know what he was talking about himself. In his gossipy way he was always referring to tax fiddles and how people had made a fortune and what price such and such a shop in the town would fetch. The fact that he'd mentioned income tax evasion in connection with the Gregarys didn't mean that there was any truth in the suggestion. Even so, the reference, coupled with the information that Mr Gregary was in the motor-components industry, established the Gregarys as people of a certain kind. Carving the turkey, my stepfather said that in his opinion Challacombe would be restored to its former splendour.

'They haven't the land,' Mr Frye pointed out, for he himself farmed eighty acres of what had once been the Challacombe estate.

'It couldn't never be the same,' Joe added.

Plates of turkey and ham were passed from hand to hand until everyone present was attended to. My mother said that people must take vegetables and start, else the food would get cold. A more lively chatter about the new people at Challacombe broke out as the cider was consumed. Two of the Gregary daughters were married and living in some other part of the country, a third one was at university. The son was the apple of his parents' eye. The father owned a grey Daimler.

The old range which had been in our kitchen all during my childhood had only the week before been replaced by a cream-coloured Aga. The acquisition of an Aga had been my mother's dream for almost as long as I could remember. I think she'd grown to hate the range, lighting it every morning with sticks and paper, the struggles she'd had with it during the war, trying to burn wood instead of coal. But I'd been sorry to see it go. I tried to stop myself being like that about things, but I couldn't help it.

'To the birthday girl,' my stepfather said, raising his glass of cider. 'Many happy returns, my best.'

It was that that I didn't care for in him: I wasn't his best, my mother was. Yet he'd say it casually, wanting to pay a compliment but overdoing it so that you didn't believe him, so that you distrusted him.

'Matilda,' other people said, holding up their glasses also. 'To Matilda.'

'Oh, my love!' my mother cried out, getting up and running round the table to kiss me. 'Oh, little Matilda!' I could feel the warm dampness of tears as her cheek came into contact with mine, and the touch of her mouth, reminding me of childhood. It was a long time since my mother had kissed me.

Everyone made a fuss then, even Martin Draper and Joe and Arthur. I can still see the sunburnt face of Colin Gregg, and his pale smooth hair, his eyes seeming to laugh at me as he wished me many happy returns. For a split second he reminded me of my father.

Betty said the turkey was delicious because she could see I was embarrassed by all the attention. Belle Frye said the next thing after a twenty-first was getting married. She reminded us that she'd been married herself within a fortnight of becoming twenty-one. She giggled and Martin Draper went red because everyone knew they'd got married in a hurry. She'd been terrified at the time of what her father would say, but to her surprise he'd taken the whole thing calmly, pointing out that there were worse than Martin Draper, reminding her that he'd just inherited the Bennett's Cross mill. It was Mrs Frye who'd been upset, unable to find consolation in her son-in-law's inheritance of a mill. Belle deserved better, she'd said.

'There's that chap on the haberdashery counter,' my stepfather said, winking his good eye all round the table, resting it for a moment on Roger Laze in order to stir up rivalry. 'Keen as mustard, that chap is.'

I knew he'd say that. As soon as Belle Frye had mentioned that the next thing after a twenty-first was a wedding I knew he'd refer to the chap on the haberdashery counter, a pimpled youth with no roof to his mouth. It was typical of my stepfather that he'd notice a counter-hand's interest in me. He'd repeatedly mentioned it before. It was typical that he'd mention it now, in public, assuming I'd be pleased that everyone should know I had an admirer, not thinking to himself that no girl would want even remotely to be associated with an unattractive shop-boy. It wasn't teasing, even though he winked: it was an attempt to be kind. My father would just have teased. He'd have made me blush and I'd have been angry and would have complained to my mother afterwards. It seemed silly now that I'd ever minded.

'Delicious, this stuffing is,' Betty said. 'Eat every scrap of your ham,' she warned one of her children, with a threat in her voice.

'Tip-top ham,' my stepfather said.

'I'll always remember the day Matilda was born,' Joe said. 'I nearly got sacked for letting a heifer wander.'

'A beautiful autumn,' Miss Pritchard said quietly, '1930.'

I was six weeks early, my mother said, a fact she'd told me before. She'd been over to Bennett's Cross in the trap and had had to pull hard on the reins when the pony had taken fright at a piece of newspaper on the road. It was that that had brought me on.

'Old Ashburton's funeral the day before,' Arthur said.

'I never knew that.' I looked at him, interested at last in the conversation, for it wasn't important that I'd been six weeks early or that the autumn had been beautiful. But it did seem strange that in all my conversations with Mrs Ashburton it had never become established that the man she talked so much about had been buried the day before my birth.

'Big old funeral,' Arthur said.

Miss Pritchard nodded and I could see the memory of it in her face. She wouldn't of course have attended it because the Ashburtons and she wouldn't have been on any kind of terms, there being nothing to connect them. She'd told me that when I'd asked her once; she'd explained that to people like the Ashburtons she'd been just a schoolteacher, adding that she'd only been invited to Mrs Ashburton's tennis party because everyone else had. But she'd have drawn the blinds of the school-house and would have waited in the gloom until the funeral had gone by.

I watched her as she ate her turkey and ham. I watched her thinking and remembering, not taking part in the conversations around her. She was slight and fragile-looking, wearing a brown suit with a necklace of beads falling on to a brown jersey. She'd retired about eighteen months ago; it was impossible to believe that we'd ever considered her unfair.

'You're looking lovely, dear,' Mrs Laze whispered across the table at me, leaning and poking her head out so that no one else would hear, for she was a woman who rarely spoke. The story was still told that she'd shot off Roger's foot during the war so that he wouldn't be called up, but now that the war was over it was increasingly difficult to visualize the scene and I began to think the rumour wasn't true. They both still said that an accident had happened when he was setting out to shoot rabbits.

'Thank you, Mrs Laze.'

I wasn't looking lovely, just ordinary in a lavender-coloured dress, my hair straight and reddish, freckles everywhere. Betty and Belle Frye were far prettier than I was, as they'd always been. And Betty's girls were prettier than I'd been at their age. My face was uninteresting, not quite plain, but too round, too lacking in special characteristics. I greatly disliked my hair and always had.

'D'you remember the day you kept us all in, Miss Pritchard?' Colin Gregg said, laughing. 'The entire top class?'

'*Long fields of barley and rye*,' Martin Draper said, laughing also. '*An abbot on an ambling pad*.'

Miss Pritchard laughed herself. She'd taught Joe and Arthur too. Roger Laze had been a favourite of hers, she'd never liked Belle Frye. She used to shout at Martin Draper because he couldn't understand things.

'Who's else for ham?' my stepfather cried out, on his feet again, waving a carving knife about. 'Ham? Turkey? Orders taken now, please. Pass up the plates, young Martin.'

'The builders moved in today,' I heard Roger Laze saying in his quiet voice, answering a question Miss Pritchard had asked him. He was referring to Challacombe Manor, and I imagined the builders shaking their heads over the place, over the broken windows and the leaking roof and the floorboards that gave way when you walked on them. 'D'you remember that day?' Belle Frye shouted down the table at me, and I smiled at her and said yes, knowing she meant the day we'd climbed in through a window.

'Go round with the cider, love,' my stepfather murmured at me because my mother and Betty were busy seeing to the vegetables.

'Oh, I'm sorry,' I whispered back at him apologetically, feeling I should have noticed that no one was attending to people's glasses.

'No matter,' he said.

I don't know what I wanted then. I don't know what birthday present I'd have awarded myself if I'd been able to, October

2nd, 1951. When I'd left the Grammar School it seemed natural to work on the farm, and I preferred it to the other occupations people suggested to me. My stepfather said he could get me into Blow's and my mother wanted me to try for a position in the accounting department of the Electricity Board because she said I was good at figures, which I wasn't. She used also to say it might be nice to be a receptionist in the Hogarth Arms Hotel. Miss Pritchard said I should become a teacher.

But I liked our farm. I liked it all the year round, the cold dairy on icy mornings, the clatter of cans and churns, driving in the cattle on a warm afternoon, working the sheepdogs. I didn't mind when the yard was thick with muck. I didn't object to the smell of silage. I even liked the hens.

Joe did all the rough work, clearing drains and the hedging and muck-spreading. My mother helped, especially at hay-making. Everyone helped then, even my stepfather; Colin Gregg and Betty came over, and the Fryes and the Lazes. More than anything else, hay-making reminded me of the past. Belle Frye and I used to run about when we were children, trying to be useful but really being a nuisance. I remembered dinnertimes, pasties and meat sandwiches in the fields, and cider and tea. My father used to eye the sky, but it always seemed to be fine then, for just long enough. 'We can laugh at it now,' he used to say when rain came and the hay was safely in.

On my twenty-first birthday I kept thinking of my mother and my stepfather becoming older in the farmhouse, my stepfather retiring from Blow's and being around all during the day. It was the same resentment I'd had of him when I was a child, before he married my mother, but of course it wasn't so intense now and it wasn't so violent. Yet it felt all wrong when I contemplated remaining with them in the farmhouse. It felt as if I'd married him too.

I opened my presents when we'd had our trifle, and I felt that everyone had been generous. Miss Pritchard had given me a cameo brooch which she used to wear herself and which I'd often admired. There were even things from Betty's children. My mother and stepfather had bought me a sewing-machine and Betty a clock for beside my bed, and Belle Frye a framed photograph of Trevor Howard, which was a joke really and typical of Belle Frye. Joe and Maudie had brought honeycombs and Mrs Laze and Roger a set of make-up and scent. There was another parcel, wrapped in red tissue paper and tied with a bow. It contained an eggcup and a matching saucer, and my stepfather said they came from the youth in Blow's. I didn't believe they did. I believed my stepfather had wrapped up the eggcup and saucer, thinking I'd be pleased if he pretended the boy had sent them. I felt awkward and embarrassed; I'd no idea what to say.

We played games with Betty's children afterwards, Snap and Snakes and Ladders. Roger Laze sat next to me, too shy to say a word; I often wondered if he was in pain from his foot. At a quarter past nine Betty and Colin Gregg had to go because it was long past their children's bedtime, and Joe and Maudie said they must be getting along also.

'So must I,' Miss Pritchard said.

She refused a lift with Colin and Betty and I said I'd like to walk with her because the night was beautiful, glaring with moonlight. I could see my mother thought I was silly to want to walk a mile and a half with an old schoolteacher who was being silly herself not to accept a lift when a lift was going. It was typical of me, my mother was thinking, like not having a more suitable twenty-first birthday party. Yet that walk through the moonlit lanes was the happiest part of it.

'Well, Matilda?' Miss Pritchard asked.

I knew what she was talking about. I said I didn't know; just stay on at the farm, I supposed.

'You'd be quite good with children, you know.'

'No.'

'Oh, well, perhaps you'll become a farmer's wife. You could do worse, I suppose.'

'I don't want to marry anyone.' The square face of Roger Laze came into my mind, and the face of the youth in Blow's. 'I really don't.'

'People often don't until someone comes along. Mr Right he's called.' Miss Pritchard laughed, and then we talked about other things, in particular about the new people at Challacombe Manor and what a difference it would make having that big old house occupied again.

Mr Gregory was a stout man and his wife was exceedingly thin. Their son was much older than I'd thought he'd be, thirty-seven as it turned out. They called him Ralphie. His brown hair was balding, and as if to make up for that he had a moustache. It was extensive but orderly, like a trimmed brown hedge in the pinkness of his face. He was broad and quite tall, rather clumsy in his movements.

All three of them came over to the farm one morning. They'd driven down from London to see how the builders were getting on and they came over to introduce themselves. Neither my mother nor I liked them.

'Cooee!' Mrs Gregory called out in our yard, standing there in unsuitable shoes and clothes. Her husband and her son were poking about the outhouses, pointing things out to one another as if they owned the place. They were dressed in tweed suits which you could see had been put on specially for the occasion; Mr Gregory carried a shooting stick.

'Forgive the intrusion!' Mrs Gregary shouted at me when I came out of the byre. Her voice was shrill, like a bird's. A smile broke her bony face in half. Her hair was very smart; her lipstick matched the maroon of the suit she was wearing.

'We're the Gregarys,' her husband said. 'Challacombe Manor.'

'This was the home-farm, wasn't it?' his son asked, more modestly than his parents might have, less casually.

I said it had been and brought them into the kitchen, not knowing what on earth else to do with them. I was wearing fawn corduroy trousers and a fawn jersey that was darned and dirty. My mother was covered in flour, making a cake at the kitchen table. She became as flustered as I'd ever seen her when I walked in with the three Gregarys.

They were totally unlike their predecessor at Challacombe Manor, seeming a different species from her. As my mother cleared away her cake-making stuff I kept imagining Mrs Ashburton frowning over the Gregarys, bewildered by them and their conversation. In a humble way that annoyed me my mother apologized because the sitting-room wasn't warm, giving the Gregarys to believe it just happened to be that on this one particular morning a fire hadn't been lit there. I don't ever remember a fire being lit in the sitting-room, which was a room that smelt of must. The only time I remember anyone sitting down in it was when my father entertained a man from the taxation authorities, going through papers with him and giving him whisky.

'Now please don't put yourselves out!' Mrs Gregary shrilled. 'Anything does for the Gregarys.'

'We've been pigging it up in the house all morning,' her husband added, and he and his wife laughed over this, finding it amusing. The son laughed less.

'You could do with tea, I'm sure,' my mother said. She was cross with me for bringing them into the kitchen to find her all red-faced and floury, but what could I have done? Her hair was untidy and she was wearing a pair of slippers. 'Put out the cups, Matilda,' she ordered, finding it hard to keep the displeasure out of her voice, worried in case the Gregarys thought it was directed at them.

'So you're a Matilda?' the woman said, smiling her bony smile. 'What an enchanting name!'

She'd sat down at the table. The two men were poking about the place, trying to work out what the kitchen had been like when the house had first been built. They murmured about an open fire and an oven in the wall. They glanced up the steep back stairs that led straight out of a corner of the kitchen. They even opened cupboards.

'There'd have been a wheel there,' the son said, pointing at the Aga, 'which you turned to operate the bellows.'

His father wasn't listening to him. 'Structurally in splendid nick,' he was saying. 'Not a dodgy wall, I'd say.'

'More than you could claim for the manor!' the woman cried, her sudden shrillness making my mother jump. 'My God, the damage!'

'It's been a long time empty,' my mother said.

'Dry rot, wet rot, you name it!' cried the woman. She had four rings on the fingers of her left hand and two on her right. It seemed a mistake of some kind that she was coming to live in Challacombe Manor, like an absurdity in a dream.

'We'll be interested in buying land,' Mr Gregary revealed. His head was very neat, with strands of hair brushed into its baldness. His face had a polished look, like faintly pink marble. The flesh of his chins didn't wobble, but was firm and polished too. His eyes had a flicker of amusement in them.

'It's Ralphie's venture really,' Mrs Gregary said. 'We'll only ever come on visits.'

'Oh no, no,' the son protested.

'Longish visits, darling.'

'We're all in love with Challacombe Manor actually,' Mr Gregary said. 'We can't resist it.'

I wanted to say I loved it too, just to make the statement and by making it to imply that my love was different from theirs. I wanted it to be clear that I had loved Challacombe Manor all my life, that I loved our farm and the gardens of Challacombe and the lanes around it, and the meadow we used to walk through on the way home from school, a journey which had been boring at the time. I wanted to say that I loved the memory of the past, of the Challacombe Mrs Ashburton had told me about, as it had been before the first of the two wars, and the memory of our family as it had been before the second. I wanted to say all that to show them how silly it was to stand there in a tweed suit and to state you were in love with a house and couldn't resist it. I wanted to belittle what wasn't real.

Politely I offered them milk and sugar, not saying anything. My mother told me to get some biscuits and Mrs Gregary said not to bother, but I got them anyway. I put some on to a plate and handed them around while my mother talked about the farmhouse and the farm. The Gregarys' son smiled at me when I held the plate out to him, and all of a sudden I was aware of a pattern of events. It seemed right that Challacombe Manor had stood there empty for so long, and Mrs Ashburton's voice echoed in my mind telling me something when I was nine. I didn't know what it was, but all the same I felt that sense was being woven into the confusion. An event had occurred that morning in the kitchen, and it seemed extraordinary that I hadn't guessed it might, that I hadn't known that this was how things were meant to be.

'They think we're peasants, finding us like this,' my mother said crossly when they'd gone.

'It doesn't matter what they think.'

A long time went by, more than a year. Challacombe Manor was put to rights. The garden was cleared of the brambles that choked it; for the second time in my memory the tennis court became a tennis court again; the masonry of the summer-house was repointed. I watched it all happening. I stood in the garden and sometimes Ralphie Gregary stood beside me, as if seeking my approval for what he was doing. I walked with him through the fields; I showed him the short-cut we'd taken every day from school, the walk through the meadow and then through the garden; I told him about the tennis party Mrs Ashburton had given on the Thursday afternoon before the second of the two wars.

One day we had a picnic, one Sunday morning. We had it in the garden, near a magnolia tree; there was white wine and chicken and tomatoes and chives, and then French cheese and grapes. He told me about the boarding-school he'd been to. When he left it he went into his father's motor-components business and then he had fought in the war. During the war he had slowly come to the conclusion that what he wanted to do when it was over was to live a quiet life. He had tried to return to his father's business but he hadn't cared for it in the least. 'This is what I like,' he said. I felt quite heady after the wine, wanting to lie down in the warmth of the noon sun. I told him how Dick and Betty and I had collected ladybirds for Mrs Ashburton so that they could eat the aphids that attacked the 65 roses. I showed him the table in the summer-house which had been laden with food on the day of the tennis party. I smiled at him and he smiled back at me, understanding my love of the past.

'You can't make it come back, you know,' Miss Pritchard pointed out to me that same day, in her tiny sitting-room.

'I hate the present.'

We ate the macaroons she'd made, and drank tea from flowered porcelain. It was all right for Miss Pritchard. Miss Pritchard was too old to belong in the present, she didn't have to worry about it.

'You mustn't hate it.' Her pale eyes were like ice, looking into mine. For a moment she was frightening, as she used to be when you didn't know something at school. But I knew she didn't mean to frighten me. 'You should love the man you marry, Matilda.'

She didn't know, she couldn't be expected to understand. Mrs Ashburton would have known at once what was in my mind.

'He says he loves me,' I said.

'That isn't the same.'

'Mrs Ashburton –'

'Oh, for heaven's sake forget her!'

I shook my head. 'It'll be all right, Miss Pritchard.' He wasn't like his parents, I tried to explain to her; he was thoughtful and much quieter than either his father or his mother. In all sorts of ways he had been kind to me; he considered me beautiful even though I was not; there was a goodness about him.

'You're doing something wrong,' Miss Pritchard said.

I shook my head again and smiled at her. Already I had persuaded Ralphie to have the drawing-room of Challacombe

66   Manor redecorated as it had been in Mrs Ashburton's time, with

the same striped red wallpaper, and brass lamps on the walls, connected now to the electricity he'd had put in. A lot of the furniture from the drawing-room was still there, stored in the cellars, locked in after Mrs Ashburton's death so that it wouldn't be stolen. It was the kind of thing that had happened in the war, a temporary measure until everyone had time to think again. No one knew who'd put it there, and some of it had suffered so much from damp that it had to be abandoned. But there were four upright armchairs, delicately inlaid, which needed only to be re-upholstered. I had them done as I remembered them, in crimson and pink stripes that matched the walls. There were the two small round mahogany tables I'd admired, and the pictures of local landscapes in heavy gilt frames, and the brass fire-irons, and Mrs Ashburton's writing-desk that had been her husband's. The pale patterned carpet came from Persia, she had told me. A corner of it had been nibbled by rats, but Ralphie said we could put a piece of furniture over the damage.

He told me he'd loved me the moment he'd seen me in our farmyard. He had closed his eyes in that moment; he had thought he was going to faint. There was no girl in England who was loved as much as I was, he said shyly, and I wondered if it would sound any different if Roger Laze had said it, or the counter-hand in Blow's. When I'd handed him the biscuits, I said, I'd felt the same; because there didn't seem any harm in saying that, in telling a minor lie in order to be kind. His parents didn't like what was happening, and my mother and stepfather didn't either. But none of that mattered because Ralphie and I were both grown-up, because Ralphie was getting on for forty and had a right to make a choice. And I intended to be good to him, to cook nice food for him and listen to his worries.

The wedding reception took place in the Hogarth Arms, although the Gregarys suggested the Bower House Hotel, twelve miles away, because there was more room there. They wanted to pay for everything, but my mother wouldn't agree to that. I suppose, in a way, it was all a bit awkward. You could feel the Gregarys thinking that my stepfather worked in a shop, that it was ridiculous of Ralphie to imagine he could take a girl from a farmyard and put her into Challacombe Manor.

Miss Pritchard came to the service and to the Hogarth Arms afterwards. Betty and Belle Frye were my matrons of honour and someone I'd never seen before was best man. I asked all sorts of people, the Fryes of course and Mrs Laze and Roger, and other people I'd been at school with, and Mrs Latham from Burrow Farm. I asked people from the shops in the town, and the people from the Hare and Hounds at Bennett's Cross, and the man from the artificial insemination centre, and Joe and Maudie, and Arthur. The Gregarys asked lots of people also, people like themselves.

I kept wanting to close my eyes as I stood in the lounge of the Hogarth Arms. I wanted to float away on the bubbles of the champagne I'd drunk. I couldn't understand why Miss Pritchard didn't see that everything was all right, that strictly speaking everything was perfect: I was there in my wedding-dress, married to Ralphie, who wasn't unkind; Challacombe Manor was as it used to be in its heyday, it was as Mrs Ashburton had known it as a bride also. Going to live there and watching over it seemed to make up for everything, for all the bad things that had happened, my father's death, and Dick's, and the arm that Mr Frye had had blown off, and Roger Laze's foot. The Fryes had sold their land to Ralphie because farming hadn't been easy since the losing of the arm. They'd be tenants in their farmhouse now for the rest of their lives, with a couple of acres they rented back from Ralphie: the arrangement suited them because there was no son to leave the farm to and they could enter old age in comfort. With the passing of time our own farm would revert to being the home-farm again, when it became too much for my mother. I couldn't help feeling that Ralphie knew it was what I wanted, and in his thoughtful kindliness had quietly brought it all about.

'Bless you, child,' my stepfather said.

I smiled at him because it was the thing to do on my wedding-day, but when he drew away his narrow face from mine after he'd kissed me I could see in it a reflection of what Miss Pritchard had said: he believed I shouldn't have married a man I didn't love, not even Ralphie, who was good and kind. It was in my mother's face too when she kissed me, and in my sister's and Belle Frye's, but not in the Gregarys' because none of them knew me.

'I'm happy,' I kept saying, smiling.

We went away to a hotel and then we came back to Challacombe. I'd almost imagined there'd be servants waiting, but of course there weren't. Instead there were the people called Stritch, a man and his wife. I'd always known the Stritches. I remembered Belle Frye and myself singing as we went by their cottage, raising our voices in a song about a bad-tempered woman because that was what Mrs Stritch was. I didn't like finding them there when we came back from our honeymoon.

There were small, silly misunderstandings between Ralphie and myself. They didn't matter because Ralphie's goodness lapped over them, and when I think about them I can't even remember very clearly what some of them were. All I can remember was that Ralphie always listened to me: I think he believed he needed to be gentle with me because I was still almost a child. I couldn't understand why he hadn't married someone before. I asked him, but he only smiled and shook his head. I had the feeling that in his mind there was the house, and the estate, and me; that I was part of the whole; that he had fallen in love with everything. All that, of course, should have been a bond between us, because the house and the estate formed the island of common ground where both of us were happy. Our marriage had Challacombe at its heart, and I was only alarmed when Ralphie spoke about our children because I didn't see that there was a need for them. Children, it seemed to me, would be all wrong. They would distort the pattern I could so precisely sense. They felt particularly alien.

Ralphie was patient with me. 'Yes, I understand,' he had said on the evening of our marriage, standing in front of me in the bedroom of the hotel he'd brought me to. The walls of the room were papered with a pinkish paper; Ralphie was wearing a flannel suit. In the hotel restaurant, called the Elizabethan Room, we had had dinner and wine. I'd had a coupe, Jacques and Ralphie some kind of apricot soufflé. 'Yes,' he said again in the pinkish bedroom, and I talked to him for ages, making him sit beside me on one of the two beds in the room, holding his hand and stroking it. 'Yes, I understand,' he said, and I really think he did; I really think he understand that there was no question of children at Challacombe. He kept saying he loved me; he would never not love me, he said.

On the evening when we returned from our honeymoon I brought up the subject of the Stritches straight away. I explained it all to Ralphie when we were having supper, but he replied that he'd told me ages ago the Stritches were going to be at Challacombe. The arrangement apparently was that Mrs Stritch would come to the house every day except Sunday, and her husband would work in the garden. Ralphie repeated most earnestly that he'd told me this before, that he'd quite often mentioned the Stritches, and had asked my opinion of them. I knew he was mistaken, but I didn't want to say so. Ralphie had a lot on his mind, buying the Fryes' land and negotiating to buy Mrs Laze's, and wondering how to go about buying my mother's. He didn't know much about farming, but he was keenly endeavouring to learn. All of it took time: he couldn't be blamed if he made little mistakes about what he'd said to me and what he hadn't.

'You see, it's awkward, Ralphie,' I explained again one night at supper, smiling at him. 'Belle Frye and I said terrible things to her.'

'Oh, Mrs Stritch'll have forgotten. Darling, it's donkeys' years ago.'

For some reason I didn't like him using that endearment, especially when he put the word at the beginning of a sentence, as he often for some reason did. I don't know why I objected so much to that. It was how it sounded, I think, a sort of casualness that seemed out of place in the house. There was another thing: he had a way of turning the pages of a newspaper, one page and then another, until finally he pored over the obituaries and the little advertisements. I didn't like the way he did that. And I didn't like the way he sometimes drummed the surface of a table with one hand when he was thinking, as if playing the piano. Another thing was, he wore leather gaiters.

'It's just that it's embarrassing for me,' I said, still smiling. 'Having her around.'

He ate beetroot and a sardine salad I had prepared because he'd told me he liked sardines. I'd made him wait that morning in the car while I went into a shop and bought several tins. I wouldn't let him see what they were, wanting it to be a surprise. He said:

'Actually, Mrs Stritch is very nice. And he's doing wonders with the garden.'

'We called her terrible names. She'd be hanging out her washing or something and we'd deliberately raise our voices. "Worst temper in Dorset," Belle would say and then we'd giggle. "Driven her husband to drink," I'd say. "Mrs Stritch is a – very nice lady," we used to call out in sing-song voices.'

'All children call people names.'

'Oh, Betty would never have let me do that. Going home from school with Betty and Dick was different. But then they left, you see. They left the Grammar when Belle and I were just finishing at Miss Pritchard's, the same time that –'

'Darling, the Stritches have to be here. We have to have help.'

'I wish you wouldn't do that, Ralphie.'

'Do what?'

'I wish you wouldn't begin a sentence like that.'

He frowned at my smile, not understanding what was in my mind even though he was an understanding person. He didn't understand when I explained that I could manage the house on my own, that I didn't need Mrs Stritch in the way. I explained to him that Mrs Stritch had once taken a pair of gloves from Blow's. 'Please let's try it,' he said, and of course I didn't want to be difficult. I wanted him to see that I was prepared to try what he wished to try.

'Yes,' I said, smiling at him.

Like a black shadow she was in the drawing-room. She leaned back in her chair, one hand stretched out to the round table in front of her. It was just a memory, not the ghost of Mrs

Ashburton, nothing like that. But the memory would have been better if Mrs Stritch hadn't always been around when Ralphie wasn't. Ralphie would go off every morning in his gaiters, and then Mrs Stritch would arrive. She would dust and clean and carry buckets of soapy water about the house. Her husband would come to the kitchen to have lunch with her, and Ralphie and I would have lunch in the dining-room. All afternoon I'd continue to be aware of her in the house, making little noises as she did her work. When it was time for her to go Ralphie would be back again.

'We're buying the Lazes' land,' he said one evening, crossing the drawing-room and pouring some whisky for himself from a decanter. I could see that he was delighted. 'I think your mother'll want to sell too,' he said.

I knew she would. Joe and Arthur were getting old, my stepfather was always saying the day would come. He'd no interest in the farm himself, and my mother would be glad not to have the responsibility.

'But you'll let the Lazes stay on in the farmhouse?' I said, because it worried me that they should have to move away.

He shook his head. He said they didn't want to. They wanted to go and live nearer the town, like the Fryes did.

'The Fryes? But the Fryes don't want to move away. You said they were going to farm a couple of acres –'

'They've changed their minds.'

I didn't smile at him any more because I didn't like what he was saying. He'd explained quite clearly that the Fryes would stay in the farmhouse, and that the Lazes could if they wanted to. He had reassured me about that. Yet he said now:

'You wanted the estate to be all together again, Matilda.'

'I didn't want people driven off, Ralphie. Not the Fryes and the Lazes. And what about my mother? Will she go also?'

'It'll be your mother's choice, Matilda. As it was theirs.'

'You've bought them all out. You promised me one thing and –'

'We need the housing for our own men.'

I felt deceived. I imagined a discussion between Ralphie and the man he'd hired to look after the estate, a cold-faced man called Epstone. I imagined Epstone saying that if you were going to do the thing, do it properly, offer them enough and they'll go. I imagined a discussion between Ralphie and his father, Ralphie asking if he could have another loan in order to plan his estate correctly, and his father agreeing.

'Well, I dare say,' I said to Ralphie, smiling at him again, determined not to be cross.

'In the old days on the Challacombe estate,' he said, 'it would have happened less humanely.'

I didn't want to hear him going on about that so I didn't ask him what he meant. Even though he was considerate, I had begun to feel I was his property. It was an odd feeling, and I think it came from the other feeling I had, that he'd married me because I was part of an idea he'd fallen in love with. I used to look at the china vases on the drawing-room mantelpiece and feel like one of them, or like the carpets and the new wallpaper. I was part of something his money had created, and I don't think he noticed that the rattling of his newspaper or the clink of the decanter against his glass had a way of interrupting my thoughts. These noises, and his footsteps in the hall or in a room, were like the noises Mrs Stritch made with her buckets and the Electrolux, but of course I never told him that.

I have forgotten a little about all that time in the house with Ralphie. He didn't always tell me what was happening on the estate; in a way he talked more readily to Mrs Stritch, for I often heard him. He also talked to himself. He would pace up and down the lawns Mr Stritch had restored, wagging his head or nodding, while I watched him from a window of the house. As time went by, it was clear that he had done what he'd wanted. As he said, the estate was all of a piece again. He had bought our farm and the farmhouse, offering so much for both that it couldn't be resisted. Joe and Arthur worked for him now.

Years were passing. Sometimes I walked over to see Miss Pritchard, going by the meadow we'd gone through on our way to school. I can't quite recall what we talked about as we had tea; only bits from our conversations come back to me. There is my own cheerfulness, my smiling at Miss Pritchard, and Miss Pritchard's glumness. Now and again I walked down to our farm and sat for a while with my mother, getting up to go before my stepfather returned. I went to see Betty and Belle, but I did that less and less. I began to think that they were all a little jealous of me. I thought that because I sensed an atmosphere when I went on these visits. 'You're cruel, Matilda,' Miss Pritchard said once, seeming to be unable to control the ill-temper that had caused the remark to surface. She turned her head away from me when she'd spoken. 'Cruel,' she said again, and I laughed because of course that was nonsensical. I remember thinking it was extra-ordinary that Miss Pritchard should be jealous.

Ralphie, I believe, must have begun to live some kind of life of his own. He often went out in the evenings, all dressed up. He came back jovial and would come to my room to kiss me good-night, until eventually I asked him not to. When I inquired at breakfast about where he'd been the night before his answer was always the same, that he had been to a house in the neighbour-hood for dinner. He always seemed surprised that I should ask the question, claiming on each occasion that he had told me these details beforehand and that I had, in fact, refused to accompany him. In all this I really do not think he can have been right.

I welcomed the occasions when Ralphie went out in the evenings. I drew the curtains in the drawing-room and sat by the fire, just happy to be there. I thought of the time when we were all together in the farmhouse, my father teasing Betty about Colin Gregg, Dick going as red as a sunset because my father mentioned an empty Woodbine packet he'd found. Every Sunday morning Ralphie went to church and since Mrs Stritch didn't come on Sundays, that was another good time. Ralphie would return and sit opposite me in the drawing-room, carving the beef I'd cooked him, looking at me now and again from his pink face, his teeth like chalk beneath the trim brown hedge of his moustache. I wanted to explain to him that I was happy in the house when Mrs Stritch wasn't there and when he wasn't there. I wanted to make him understand that old Mrs Ashburton had wanted me to be in her house, that that was why she had told me so much when I was a child, that everything had to do with the two wars there'd been. He didn't know as much about war as Mrs Ashburton had, even though he'd fought in one: I wanted to explain that to him, too. But I never did because his eyes would have begun to goggle, which they had a way of doing if something he couldn't comprehend was put to him. It was easier just to cook his meals and smile at him.

There was another thing Ralphie said I had forgotten: a conversation about a party he gave. When I asked him afterwards he repeatedly assured me we'd had a conversation about it, and in all honesty I believe it must have been his own memory that was at fault. Not that it matters in the least which way round it was. What mattered at the time was that the house was suddenly full of people. I was embroidering in the drawing-room, slowly stitching the eye of a peacock, and the next thing was that Ralphie's parents were embracing me, pretending they liked me. It seemed they had come for the weekend, so that they could be at the party, which was to be on the following night. They brought other people with them in their grey Daimler, people called Absom. Mrs Absom was thin, like Mrs Gregary, but younger than Mrs Gregary. Mr Absom was stout, like Mr Gregary, but not like polished marble, and younger also.

Mrs Stritch's daughter Nellie came to help on the Saturday morning and stayed all day. Apparently Ralphie had given Mrs Stritch money to buy navy-blue overalls for both of them so that they'd stand out from the guests at the party. They bought them in Blow's, Mrs Stritch told me, and it was quite funny to think that my stepfather might have served them, even fitted them with the overalls. Mr Stritch was there on the night of the party also, organizing the parking of cars.

It all took place in the drawing-room. People stood around with drinks in their hands. Ralphie introduced them to me, but I found it hard to know what to say to them. It was his mother, really, who gave the party, moving about the drawing-room as if she owned it. I realized then why she'd come for the weekend.

'So how do you like Challacombe Manor, Mrs Gregary?' a man with very short hair asked me.

Politely I replied that I was very fond of the house.

'Ralphie!' the man said, gesturing around him. 'Fantastic!' He added that he enjoyed life in the country, and told me the names of his dogs. He said he liked fishing and always had.

There were fifty-two people in the drawing-room, which had begun to smell of cigarette smoke and alcohol. It was hot because Mrs Gregary had asked Mrs Stritch to make up an   77 enormous fire, and it was becoming noisier because as the party advanced people talked more loudly. A woman, wearing a coffee-coloured dress, appeared to be drunk. She had sleek black hair and kept dropping her cigarette on to Mrs Ashburton's Persian carpet. Once when she bent to pick it up she almost toppled over.

'Hullo,' a man said. 'You're Mrs Ralphie.'

He was younger than the short-haired man. He stood very close to me, pressing me into a corner. He told me his name but I didn't listen because listening was an effort in the noisy room.

'Ever been there?' this man shouted at me. 'Ferns magnificent, this time of year.'

He smiled at me, revealing jagged teeth. 'Ferns,' he shouted, and then he said that he, or someone, had a collection of stuffed birds. I could feel one of his knees pressing into the side of my leg. He asked me something and I shook my head again. Then he went away.

Mrs Stritch and her daughter had covered the dining-room table with food. All kinds of cold meats there were, and various salads, and tarts of different kinds, and huge bowls of whipped cream, and cheeses. They'd done it all at the direction of Mrs Gregary: just by looking at the table you could see Mrs Gregary's hand in it, Mrs Stritch wouldn't have known a thing about it. The sideboard was entirely taken up with bottles of wine and glasses. The electric light wasn't turned on; there were slender red candles everywhere, another touch of Mrs Gregary's, or even Mrs Absom's. I had crossed the hall to the dining-room in order to get away from the noise for a moment. I thought I'd sit there quietly for a little; I was surprised to see the food and the candles.

I was alone in the dining-room, as I'd guessed I would be.

But it wasn't any longer a room you could be quiet in. Everything seemed garish, the red glitter of the wine bottles, the red candles, dish after dish of different food, the cheeses. It made me angry that Mrs Gregary and Mrs Absom should have come to Challacombe Manor in order to instruct Mrs Stritch, that Mrs Gregary should strut about in the drawing-room, telling people who she was.

I jumbled the food about, dropping pieces of meat into the bowls of cream, covering the tarts with salad. I emptied two wine bottles over everything, watching the red stain spreading on the tablecloth and on the cheeses. They had no right to be in the house, their Daimler had no right to be in the garage. I had asked years ago that Mrs Stritch should not be here.

In the drawing-room someone said to me:

'I enjoy to get out after pheasants, to tramp with my dogs.'

It was the short-haired man. I hadn't noticed that he was a foreigner. I knew before he told me that he was German.

'You have dogs, Mrs Gregary?'

I smiled at him and shook my head. It seemed extraordinary that there should be a German in this drawing-room. I remembered when Mrs Ashburton used to talk to me about the First World War that I'd imagined the Germans as grey and steel-like, endlessly consuming black bread. This man didn't seem in the least like that.

'Hasenfuss,' he said. 'The name, you know.'

For a moment the room was different. People were dancing there at some other party. A man was standing near the door, waiting for someone to arrive, seeming a little anxious. It was all just a flash, as if I had fallen asleep and for a moment had had a dream.

'We are enemies and then we are friends. I advise on British 79 beer, I enjoy your British countryside. It is my profession to advise on British beer. I would not enjoy to live in Germany today, Mrs Gregary.'

'You are the first German I have ever met.'

'Oh, I hope not the last.'

Again the drawing-room was different. There was the music and the dancing and the man by the door. The girl he was waiting for arrived. It was Mrs Ashburton, as she was in the photographs she'd showed me when I was nine. And he was the man she'd married.

'Here I am standing,' said the short-haired German, 'in the house of the people who put Mr Hitler in his place.' He laughed loudly when he'd made that remark, displaying more gold fillings than I had ever before seen in anyone's mouth. 'Your father-in-law, you know, made a lot of difference to the war.'

I didn't know what he was talking about. I was thinking of the dining-room and what would happen when everyone walked into it. It was like something Belle Frye and I might have done together, only we'd never have had the courage. It was worse than singing songs outside Mrs Stritch's cottage.

'In that I mean,' the German said, 'the manufacturing of guns.'

I hadn't known that. My stepfather had said that the Gregarys had made a killing, but I hadn't thought about it. Ralphie had never told me that his father's motor-components business had made guns during the war, that the war had made him rich. It was the war that enabled Ralphie now to buy up all the land and set the Challacombe estate to rights again. It was the war that had restored this drawing-room.

'The world is strange,' the German said.

I went upstairs and came down with Ralphie's gaiters. I

remember standing at the door of the drawing-room, looking at all the people drinking, and seeing again, for an instant, the dancers of the distant past. Mrs Ashburton and her husband were among them, smiling at one another.

I moved into the room and when I reached the fireplace I threw the gaiters on to the flames. Someone noticed me, Mrs Absom, I think it was. She seemed quite terrified as she watched me.

The German was again alone. He told me he enjoyed alcohol, emphasizing this point by reaching his glass out towards Mrs Stritch, who was passing with some mixture in a jug. I told him about Mrs Ashburton's husband, how he had returned from the first of the two wars suffering from shell-shock, how the estate had fallen to bits because of that, how everything had had to be mortgaged. I was telling her story, and I was even aware that my voice was quite like hers, that I felt quite like her as well. Everything had happened all over again, I told the German, the repetition was cloying. I told him about Mrs Ashburton's law of averages, how some men always came back from a war, how you had to pray it would be the men who were closest to you, how it would have been better if her own husband had been killed.

The smell of burning leather was unpleasant in the room. People noticed it. Ralphie poked at his smouldering gaiters with a poker, wondering why they were there. I saw his mother looking at me while I talked to the German. 'Mrs Ashburton did what she could,' I said. 'There's nothing wrong with living in the past.'

I went around from person to person then, asking them to go. The party had come to an end, I explained, but Mrs Gregary tried to contradict that. 'No, no, no,' she cried. 'We've scarcely started.' She ushered people into the dining-room and then, of course, she saw that I was right.

'I would like you to go as well,' I said to Mr Gregary in the hall, while the visitors were rooting for their coats. 'I would like you to go and take the Absoms with you. I did not invite the Absoms here any more than I invited you.' I said it while smiling at him, so that he could see I wasn't being quarrelsome. 'Oh now, look here, Matilda!' he protested.

In the kitchen I told Mrs Stritch that I'd rather she didn't return to the house. I could easily manage on my own, I explained to her, trying to be kind in how I put it. 'It's just that it's embarrassing,' I said, 'having you here.'

The Gregarys and the Absoms didn't go until the following day, a Sunday. They didn't say goodbye to me, and I only knew that they had finally departed because Ralphie told me. 'Why are you doing this?' he said, sitting down on the other side of the fire in the drawing-room, where I was embroidering my peacocks. 'Why, Matilda?' he said again.

'I don't understand you.'

'Yes, you do.'

He had never spoken like that before. All his considerateness had disappeared. His eyes were fiery and yet cold. His large hands looked as though they wanted to commit some act of violence. I shook my head at him. He said:

'You're pretending to be deranged.'

I laughed. I didn't like him sitting opposite me like that, with his eyes and his hands. Everything about him had been a pretence: all he wanted was his own way, to have his mother giving parties in my drawing-room, to have Mrs Stritch forever vacuuming the stairs, to own me as he owned the land and the farms and the house. It was horrible, making money out of war.

'You don't even cook for me,' he said to my astonishment. 'Half-raw potatoes, half-raw chops –'

'Oh, Ralphie, don't be silly. You know I cook for you.'

'The only food that is edible in this house is made by Mrs Stritch. You can cook if you want to, only you can't be bothered.'

'I do my best. In every way I do my best. I want our marriage to be –'

'It isn't a marriage,' he said. 'It's never been a marriage.'

'We were married in the church.'

'Stop talking like that!' He shouted at me again, suddenly on his feet, looking down at me. His face was red with fury; I thought he might pick something up and hit me with it.

'I'm sorry,' I said.

'You're as sane as I am. For God's sake, Matilda!'

'Of course I'm sane,' I said quietly. 'I could not be sitting here if I were not. I could not live a normal life.'

'You don't live a normal life.' He was shouting again, stamping about the room like an animal. 'Every second of every day is devoted to the impression you wish to give.'

'But, Ralphie, why should I wish to give an impression?'

'To cover up your cruelty.'

I laughed again, gently so as not to anger him further. I remember Miss Pritchard saying I was cruel, and of course there was the cruelty Mrs Ashburton had spoken of, the cruelty that was natural in wartime. I had felt it in myself when my father had been killed, and when Dick had been killed. I had felt it when I had first seen my mother embracing the man who became my stepfather, too soon after my father had died. God, if He existed, I had thought in the end, was something to be frightened of.

'The war is over,' I said, and he looked at me, startled by that remark.

83

'It isn't for you,' he said. 'It'll never be for you. It's all we ever hear from you, the war and that foolish old woman –'

'It wasn't over for Mrs Ashburton either. How could it be when she lived to see it all beginning again?'

'Oh, for God's sake, stop talking about her. If it hadn't been for her, if she hadn't taken advantage of a nine-year-old child with her rubbish, you would be a normal human being now.' He stood above my chair again, pushing his red face down at me and speaking slowly. 'She twisted you, she filled you full of hate. Whatever you are now, that dead woman has done to you. Millions have suffered in war,' he suddenly shouted. 'Who's asking you to dwell on it, for God's sake?'

'There are people who find it hard to pick up the pieces. Because they're made like that.'

'You'd have picked them up if she hadn't prevented you. She didn't want you to, because she couldn't herself.' Furiously he added, 'Some kind of bloody monster she was.'

I didn't reply to any of that. He said, with a bitterness in his voice which had never been there before, 'All I know is that she has destroyed Challacombe for me.'

'It was never real for you, Ralphie. I shall never forget the happiness in our farmhouse. What memories of Challacombe can you have?'

But Ralphie wasn't interested in the happiness in our farmhouse, or in memories he couldn't have. All he wanted to do was wildly to castigate me.

'How can I live here with you?' he demanded in a rough, hard voice, pouring at the same time a glass of whisky for himself. 'You said you loved me once. Yet everything you do is calculated to let me see your hatred. What have I done,' he shouted at me, 'that you hate me, Matilda?'

I quietly replied that he was mistaken. I protested that I did not hate him, but even as I spoke I realized that that wasn't true. I hated him for being what he was, for walking with his parents into the farmyard that morning, for thinking he had a place in the past. I might have confided in him but I did not want to. I might have said that I remembered, years ago, Miss Pritchard coming to see my mother and what Miss Pritchard had said. I had eavesdropped on the stairs that led to the kitchen, while she said she believed there was something the matter with me. It was before the death of Dick, after I'd discovered about my mother and the man who was now my stepfather. 'She dwells on her father's death,' Miss Pritchard had said and she'd gone on to say that I dwelt as well on the conversations I'd had with old Mrs Ashburton. I remembered the feeling I'd had, standing there listening: the feeling that the shell-shock of Mr Ashburton, carried back to Challacombe from the trenches in 1917, had conveyed itself in some other form to his wife, that she, as much as he, had been a victim of violence. I felt it because Miss Pritchard was saying something like it to my mother. 'There are casualties in wars,' she said, 'thousands of miles from where the fighting is.' She was speaking about me. I'd caught a mood, she said, from old Mrs Ashburton, and when my mother replied that you couldn't catch a mood like you caught the measles Miss Pritchard sharply replied that you could. '*Folie à deux* the French call it,' she insisted, an expression I welcomed and have never since forgotten. There had been *folie à deux* all over this house, and in the garden too, when he came back with his mind in pieces. She had shared the horror with him and later she had shared it with me, as if guessing that I, too, would be a casualty. As long as I lived I would honour that *folie* in their house. I would honour her and her husband, and my father and Dick, 85 and the times they had lived in. It was right that the cruelty was there.

'Of course I don't hate you,' I said again. 'Of course not, Ralphie.'

He did not reply. He stood in the centre of the drawing-room with his glass in his hand, seeming like a beast caught in a snare: he had all the beaten qualities of such an animal. His shoulders slouched, his eyes had lost their fire.

'I don't know what to do,' he said.

'You may stay here,' I said, 'with me.' Again I smiled, wishing to make the invitation seem kind. I could feel no pity for him.

'How could I?' he shouted. 'My God, how could I? I lose count of the years in this house. I look at you every day, I look at your eyes and your hair and your face, I look at your hands and your fingernails, and the arch of your neck. I love you; every single inch of you I love. How can I live here and love you like that, Matilda? I shared a dream with you, Matilda, a dream that no one else but you would have understood. I longed for my quiet life, with you and with our children. I married you out of passion and devotion. You give me back nothing.'

'You married me because I was part of something, a part of the house and the estate –'

'That isn't true. That's a rubbishy fantasy; not a word of it is true.'

'I cannot help it if I believe it.' I wasn't smiling now. I let my feelings show in my eyes because there was no point in doing otherwise any more. Not in a million years would he understand. 'Yes, I despise you,' I said. 'I have never felt affection for you.'

I said it calmly and bent my head again over my embroidery.

He poured more whisky and sat down in the chair on the other side of the fireplace. I spoke while still embroidering, magenta thread in a feather of my peacock's tail.

'You must never again touch me,' I said. 'Not even in passing me by in a room. We shall live here just as we are, but do not address me with endearments. I shall cook and clean, but there shall be no parties. Your parents are not welcome. It is discourteous to me to give parties behind my back and to employ people I do not care for.'

'You were told, you know perfectly well you were told –'

'You will fatten and shamble about the rooms of this house. I shall not complain. You will drink more whisky, and perhaps lose heart in your dream. "His wife does not go out," people will say; "they have no children. He married beneath him, but it isn't that that cut him down to size."'

'Matilda, please. Please for a moment listen to me –'

'Why should I? And why should you not lose heart in your dream because isn't your dream ridiculous? If you think that your Challacombe estate is like it was, or that you in your vulgarity could ever make it so, then you're the one who is deranged.'

I had not taken my eyes from the peacock's tail. I imagined a patch of damp developing on the ceiling of an upstairs room. I imagined his lifting the heavy lead-lined hatch in the loft and stepping out on to the roof to find the missing tile. I stood with him on the roof and pointed to the tile, lodged in a gutter. I had removed it myself and slid it down the incline of the roof. He could reach it with an effort, by grasping the edge of the chimney-stack to be safe. I heard the thump of his body as it struck the cobbles below. I heard it in the drawing-room as I worked my stitches, while he drank more whisky and for a while was silent.

'Damn you,' he shouted in the end, once more on his feet and seething above me. 'Damn you to hell, Matilda.'

'No matter what you do,' I said, still sewing the magenta thread, 'I shall not leave this house.'

He sold everything he'd bought except the house and garden. He sold the land and the farmhouses, the Fryes' and the Lazes' and what had been ours. He didn't tell me about any of it until he'd done it. 'I'll be gone in a week,' he said one day, six or seven months after we'd had that quarrel, and I did not urge him to stay.

It is a long time ago now, that day. I can't quite remember Ralphie's going, even though with such vividness I remember so much else. There are new people in all the farmhouses now, whole families have grown up; again the tennis court is over-grown. Miss Pritchard died, of course, and my mother and stepfather. I never saw much of them after Ralphie went and I never laid eyes on Ralphie or even had a line from him. But if Ralphie walked in now I would take his hand and say I was sorry for the cruelty that possessed me and would not go away, the cruelty she used to talk about, a natural thing in wartime. It lingered and I'm sorry it did, and perhaps after all this time Ralphie would understand and believe me, but Ralphie, I know, will never return.

I sit here now in her drawing-room, and may perhaps become as old as she was. Sometimes I walk up to the meadow where the path to school was, but the meadow isn't there any more. There are rows of coloured caravans, and motor-cars and shacks. In the garden I can hear the voices of people drifting down to me, and the sound of music from their wireless sets. Nothing is like it was.